Peekaboo. I see you.

Clint stared at the words. What the hell? What did that mean?

With a bit of unease, he unlocked his front door and stepped inside. He walked into the living room and was surprised that Lizzy wasn't there on the sofa. Maybe she'd decided to crawl into his bed to sleep, he thought.

He walked down the hallway to his bedroom, but Lizzy wasn't there, either. A bit of anxiety swept through him. She had to be here somewhere. Her truck was still outside. He peeked into Emily's room and terror gripped his heart, his very soul. Emily wasn't there. Her bed was empty.

What in the hell was going on? "Lizzy," he yelled. He waited, but there was no response. "Lizzy," he shouted even louder. Where were they? Where could they be? Dear God, what was happening?

His text alert went off again. He yanked the phone out of his pocket.

Welcome to your nightmare.

Dear Reader,

Through the years, my husband and I have had some great neighbors. They've been barbecue buddies and good friends. When we would eventually get new ones, I remember watching as their things were unloaded from a moving van and wondering if we'd become friends, as well.

Living in the country, neighbors are particularly important. They not only offer friendship but also first aid, help and other things needed in an emergency.

When Lizzy Maxwell gets a new neighbor, she's vaguely curious about him. She's unaware of how much Clint Kincaid and his little girl, Emily, are going to change her life.

I hope you enjoy this one and keep reading!

Carla Cassidy

THE COWBOY
NEXT DOOR

———

Carla Cassidy

HARLEQUIN®
ROMANTIC SUSPENSE™

Recycling programs
for this product may
not exist in your area.

ISBN-13: 978-1-335-59375-7

The Cowboy Next Door

Harlequin Enterprises ULC
22 Adelaide St. West, 41st Floor
Toronto, Ontario M5H 4E3, Canada
www.Harlequin.com

Printed in U.S.A.

A *New York Times* bestselling author, **Carla Cassidy** loves danger...but only when it comes in the pages of a book. She's been a professional cheerleader, a singer and a dancer, but the best job she's ever had is writing books for readers to enjoy. She's had over 150 books published and has enough ideas for new books to keep her busy for years to come.

Books by Carla Cassidy

Harlequin Romantic Suspense

The Scarecrow Murders

Killer in the Heartland
Guarding a Forbidden Love
The Cowboy Next Door

Colton 911: Chicago

Colton 911: Guardian in the Storm

Cowboys of Holiday Ranch

Sheltered by the Cowboy
Guardian Cowboy
Cowboy Defender
Cowboy's Vow to Protect
The Cowboy's Targeted Bride
The Last Cowboy Standing

Colton 911

Colton 911: Target in Jeopardy

Visit the Author Profile page at Harlequin.com for more titles.

Chapter 1

Lizzy Maxwell stepped outside into the intense heat of the last day of August. She turned on her heels and closed the stable doors. All the horses now had newly mucked stalls waiting for them and Lizzy's stomach told her it was near dinnertime. Another quiet, lonely meal for one.

At thirty-three years old, she'd expected to be married by now, but she'd spent two years nursing her ill father and after he passed, she'd realized in those two years a lot of the available men in town had married and started families of their own.

She headed toward the ranch house where she'd lived all her life. Thankfully her father had left her not only the house but also all the land that allowed her to keep a profitable field of corn, another of wheat, and a herd of cattle and a couple of horses. There was also a huge garden that grew all kinds of vegetables that she enjoyed eating throughout the summer.

A dust devil kicked up in the pasture in the distance, whirling for a moment and then disappearing. They were occasional sights in the summer heat here in the middle of the country. Lately she felt like one of those dust demons, whirling and twirling and somehow getting nowhere.

She had just reached her back door when she heard the sound of a horse. She turned and saw her new neighbor riding down the fence line that divided the two properties.

He was tall in the saddle with broad shoulders and long legs. It was impossible to tell his hair color as she'd only seen him when he wore a black cowboy hat.

He didn't really look like an experienced horseback rider to her. Even from this distance, he looked stiff and uncomfortable. He'd moved in two months before and she had yet to officially meet him.

All she knew was that his name was Clint Kincaid, he was divorced and had a five-year-old daughter. She'd heard that from Mildred Hunter who worked at the post office. There had been no real gossip about him. From what little Mildred said, he pretty much stayed to himself and hadn't spent much of any time in town since moving in.

Of course, Millsville, Kansas, didn't have a lot to

offer in the way of entertainment unless you wanted to hang out at one of the two bars in town. There was no movie theatre or fancy restaurants; however there were the usual amenities of a small town. The café was a great place to eat and recently a beautiful gazebo had been built in the town square. It boasted lots of benches where people could sit and visit.

Lizzy loved it here, where the air was clean and she could ride across her pastures whenever she wanted or throw a fishing pole into her large pond, where the catfish were almost always biting.

The crunch of tires on gravel turned her in the opposite direction. A smile curved her lips as she saw the familiar red Mustang convertible driving up her driveway.

Bailey Troy, the owner of the car, was a force of nature. She owned the Sassy Nails Salon, a place where women went not only to get manicures and pedicures but also to drink a glass of champagne and gossip. She had also been Lizzy's best friend since their early high school days.

Her short, spiked blond hair sparkled in the sunshine and her gold-rimmed sunglasses threatened to swallow up her petite, gamin features.

She pulled up and parked and then got out of the car and grinned at Lizzy. "Want to head to the café for an early dinner?" Bailey asked. She pulled her sunglasses off and dropped them into her oversize blingy, pink purse, exposing her bright blue eyes.

Lizzy shook her head. "Instead of going to the

café, why don't you come into Chez Lizzy's and have an early dinner here with me instead?"

"What's on the menu?" Bailey asked.

"Crock-Pot chicken stuff," Lizzy replied. "The company is good, the meal is free and should be pleasantly edible."

"Sold," Bailey said. Together the two women headed for the front door. Just before walking in, Lizzy cast a quick gaze at her neighbor's place, but she saw no sign of him anymore.

"Have you met him yet?" Bailey asked as they walked through the living room and into the bright, airy kitchen.

"Who?" Lizzy asked. She went directly onto the screened-in back porch and kicked off her boots, then she padded back into the kitchen.

"The new guy…your neighbor." Bailey sat at the wooden table and then dropped her purse on the floor next to her.

"Not officially, although I've seen him out and about on his place. Why?" She washed her hands and then got a couple of plates out of the cabinet.

"I saw him in town yesterday. He was going into the feed store. He's definitely a hottie."

Lizzy set the plates on the table and then added silverware. "I heard he's divorced, so he's free for you to go after."

"No thanks. He's definitely not my type. Can I do anything to help?"

"No, just sit and relax, I've got it. So, why is he

not your type?" Lizzy continued to set the table with a salad she'd made earlier in the day, the chicken and veggies from the Crock-Pot and iced tea to drink.

"First of all, he's got a kid and you know that I'm not ready to be a mommy or step-mommy anytime soon. Secondly, he has dark hair and I've always been partial to blond guys."

"You mean blonds like Officer Benjamin Cooper?" Lizzy asked as she finally sat at the table across from her friend. She laughed as Bailey's cheeks turned a pretty shade of pink.

"You've got to admit it, Benjamin Cooper is one fine-looking man." Bailey scooped some of the chicken onto her plate.

"Bailey, you've had a crush on him forever. What I don't understand is why you haven't made a move on him yet? You know you aren't getting any younger."

"Thanks for reminding me of that," Bailey said dryly. "Every time I get close to him my stomach clenches and the back of my throat closes up. Besides, I think he's seeing Celeste Winthrop right now, and if she's the type of woman he likes, then he's definitely not the right man for me."

Celeste Winthrop was a divorcée who was hungry for another husband. She was a pretty woman on the outside, but inside she was known to be arrogant and condescending to other women.

For the next hour they ate and gossiped about various people in town. "I think Laura Dean is going to leave her husband," Bailey said.

"Really? I always thought she was happy with Ralph," Lizzy replied. "They always seem happy together when I see them out and about."

"I guess nobody really knows what goes on behind closed doors." Bailey's eyes darkened. "Just think, somebody is behind one right now, plotting another scarecrow murder."

A whisper of a chill slithered up Lizzy's back. "I don't even like to think about it."

"Lizzy, we have to think about it. We're both blondes with blue eyes…just like the last two women he killed. We're his type. I worry about you because you live out here all alone."

"And I worry about you because you live and work in town. He would see you way more than he would see me since I don't go into town too often." Lizzy fought against another chill.

There was a serial killer at work in the small Kansas town of Millsville. He'd been dubbed the Scarecrow Killer because he dressed up his victims like human scarecrows. He sewed their mouths shut with thick black thread, dressed them in jeans, a plaid shirt and a straw hat and then trussed them up on a pole like a true scarecrow. It was all very creepy, but the creepiest thing of all was that he took his victims' eyes.

The police chief had tried to keep that particular thing under wraps, but somebody had leaked the information and it had since made the rounds through gossip, terrifying every young woman.

The first victim had been Cindy Perry, a pleasant young woman who had worked as a waitress at the café. She'd been found in a farmer's cornfield. The second victim had been Sandy Blackstone, who had been a teller at the bank. Her body had been found in the backyard of the Sweet Tooth Bakery. Both had possessed blond hair and blue eyes.

There was now a new tension in the air… It was the apprehension of everyone waiting for another victim to show up. So far, the chief of police, Dallas Calloway, had no clues and no suspects in the case.

"Let's change the subject, otherwise I'm going to have a bad case of indigestion," Bailey said. She reached across the table and grabbed Lizzy's hand in hers. "When are you going to come into the shop and get your nails done by me?"

Lizzy pulled her hand away and laughed. "First of all, your nail art scares me to death. Secondly, it's impractical for me to wear fancy nails around the ranch."

"So, be impractical for once in your life, Lizzy Maxwell. I promise I won't paint a space alien or cornstalks on them. What you should do is let me paint them a bright red, and you pull on that red swirl skirt you have and you take some of your bright red cupcakes to your neighbor."

Lizzy laughed once again. "And why would I want to do something like that?"

"Because you're ready for a husband and he's a new guy in town and you never know if he's the one for you or not," Bailey replied. "Besides, since you're on the city council, it would be the neighborly thing for you to do."

"Ugh, don't remind me of the city council. Right now, I'm enemy number one with all the other members."

"Why is that?" Bailey asked curiously.

"It's budget time and I swear the other members have lost their ever-loving minds. They want to pass a huge budget that will make all of our taxes go up and I just don't believe now is the time to do it. Since our constitution states the budget vote has to be unanimous, all the other members see me as the devil himself right now, because I couldn't vote yes on the one they wanted."

Lizzy got up from the table and grabbed their now-empty plates. "All I really want is for some compromises to be made and then I'd be all in."

"And I need to gather all my strength tonight because my first customer of the day tomorrow is Letta Lee." Bailey grabbed the dirty silverware and glasses from the table and carried them to the sink.

"Ugh, lucky you. And guess who asked for a ton of money in the town's budget for the woman's gardening club," Lizzy replied.

"Let me guess...the same arrogant, hateful, old witch whose nails I'm painting in the morning," Bailey said. "By the way, thanks for dinner. That Crock-Pot stuff was the bomb."

"It's easy to make. I try to Crock-Pot a meal a couple of times a week. After working hard around here, it's nice to have the meal ready to eat."

"For me, it's way easier to grab a burger or some chicken fingers on the way home from work," Bailey replied.

"I'm not driving all the way into town to eat chicken fingers after a long day's work," Lizzy protested.

With the dishes all cleaned up, the two moved into the living room. "It's been two years since your daddy passed and you need to start putting yourself out there more," Bailey said.

"Put myself out there more?" Lizzy looked at her friend in disbelief. "I'm already on the city council and I volunteer at the food bank. I also work this place. What else do you want me to do?"

"I don't know… Maybe it's time we both go back to the bar scene. Most of the single guys in town hang out at Murphy's on the weekends."

"Yuck, you know how much I absolutely hate the bar scene," Lizzy replied.

"I know how picky you are when it comes to men," Bailey said.

"I'm not picky, I just know what I want," Lizzy said in her own defense.

"You'll never find him, Lizzy. You're looking for Mr. Perfect and he just doesn't exist," Bailey said.

"Then I'll be single for the rest of my life."

"But I know you get lonely," Bailey said softly. "Who knows? Maybe your Mr. Right, dream man is two-stepping it away right now at Murphy's."

"I'm too tired in the evenings to go dancing," Lizzy said.

"While we're on that topic, when are you going to hire some help around here? I know your dad didn't want anyone else working the ranch, but you do realize this place is too big for one person to handle."

Lizzy released a deep sigh. "I'll admit it's been a struggle to keep up with things around here. I know I need to hire a couple of men to help me out, but I just haven't been in the mood to start the whole interview process."

"Put an ad in the paper or wherever and once you have things set up, I'll help you interview the men," Bailey offered.

"Yeah, right," Lizzy said with a laugh. "And what do you know about the ranching business?"

"I know the criteria for a ranch hand," Bailey replied with one of her naughty grins. "To start with, they have to have really broad shoulders and tight butts."

"Bailey," Lizzy said with yet another laugh. "You are incorrigible."

Bailey grinned at her and then stood. "This incorrigible woman is now getting out of here so you can relax for the rest of the evening. Lunch tomorrow?"

"Sure. What time?" Lizzy walked her friend to the front door.

"Noon at the café."

"Okay, I'll see you then."

Lizzy watched as Bailey got into her car and then

roared down the driveway. Although she wasn't big on going into town for lunch, she knew she had to compromise occasionally and couldn't always expect Bailey to drive out to her place. Before she closed the door completely, she glanced over to the ranch house in the distance.

Maybe it would be a nice thing to do, to bake some cupcakes or cookies and welcome the new neighbors. However, she certainly wasn't going to get her nails painted a fire-engine red or pull on the flirty red skirt that she'd worn occasionally to Murphy's Bar.

It would just be a quick visit to introduce herself and welcome him to town and nothing more. If she decided to do it at all.

"Daddy?" Emily looked up from the piece of paper she'd been drawing and coloring on. "I gotta question. Can I ask you something?"

Clint Kincaid sat next to his five-year-old daughter at the kitchen table. He smiled at her. "Anytime and anywhere, you can always ask me a question. Even if I'm standing on my head, you can ask me a question."

Emily giggled, which was the exact response he was hoping to get. She then sobered and her bright blue eyes gazed at him seriously. "How come Amy Pearson had two mommies and I don't have a single one? That doesn't seem fair to me."

"Amy has two mothers, but if you remember she didn't have a father. So, it is kind of fair," he replied.

Amy had been Emily's friend six months ago when they'd both been in the same kindergarten together.

"I guess," Emily said reluctantly. "I still would like to have a mommy."

"You had a wonderful mommy," Clint said, the memory of his late wife shooting a quick, sharp pain through his heart. "She loved you very, very much. I know even now she's looking down on you from heaven and she's still loving you with all her heart."

"That's good. I love my mommy in heaven. Look, Daddy, I colored our new house with you and me in the front yard." She picked up the paper to display to him her work of art.

"That's beautiful, bug. Why don't we put it on the refrigerator door with all the others? And then it's time for bath and bed," he replied.

"'Kay," she replied.

Thankfully Emily never fought with him about taking a bath, but bedtime was sometimes another matter. "Butterfly or ladybug?" he asked as he picked up the small container on the cabinet next to the refrigerator.

"Ladybug," she replied.

He grabbed two of the ladybug-shaped magnets from the container and used them to hang the drawing. "It looks beautiful here with all the other ones. I love to see your artwork here. Now, it's time to get into the tub."

Fifteen minutes later Emily was in a bubble bath and Clint returned to the kitchen table to finish his cup of coffee. The sound of Emily singing and splashing in the tub brought another smile to his lips. She was like a little fish.

He'd been a single father since Emily was almost two. He'd learned a lot of things about raising a little girl by trial and error, but she seemed to be thriving beneath his care and that's all he cared about.

He felt like he'd been in hell for a very long time. He hadn't been at peace for an equally long time. Finally he believed he was in a place where he could relax and breathe. Surely nobody would come looking for them on a ranch in this small Kansas town.

Within thirty minutes Emily was bathed and in bed. As was their usual custom, Clint sat on the edge of the mattress for a nighttime story or two before the lamp on the bedside table was turned off.

"Last night I told you a story about Bert the Bee, so I think it's your turn to tell me a story tonight," he said to her.

"'Kay." Her little nose wrinkled with her concentration. "There once was a flea named Freddy and he used to live in the pretty, soft fur of a sweet little dog named Fifi."

"Fifi? That's a nice name," Clint said.

"Daddy," she said and then paused and smiled her most charming little smile. "If I can't have a mommy, then I think it's only fair that I get a puppy and we could name her Fifi. What do you think about that idea, huh, Daddy?"

Clint laughed. "I think Daddy needs some more time to think about getting a dog."

Emily placed her small palm on the side of his face. "How much more time, Daddy?" she asked winsomely.

"I should have an answer for you by your birthday in three weeks," he replied.

"Will it be a good birthday or a bad birthday?"

He laughed once again. "Whether I agree to get a dog or not, we're going to have a great birthday. I've got a special surprise planned for a special little girl."

"For me," she squealed, her eyes shining with excitement.

"That's right, but now you need to go to sleep so you can have a great first day of school tomorrow morning."

"Will I make new friends there?" Emily asked hopefully.

Clint's heart squeezed tight. He knew how lonely his daughter had been without any relatives or friends. They had never really been settled in one place long enough for her to make many friends.

"You're going to make lots and lots of new friends," he assured her. He leaned over and kissed her on the forehead. "Kisses to the moon and back, that's how much I love you," he said softly.

"Night, Daddy. I love you much and much and more." She snuggled down into the pink sheets and within minutes she was sound asleep.

Clint turned off the lamp on her nightstand,

plunging the room into a semidarkness except for the glow created by a strong nightlight.

He remained in the doorway gazing at the precious little girl. Life had been beyond chaotic for her as they had hopped around from place to place. He hoped they could stay here, at least for a while. She needed friends. She needed some semblance of normalcy. Hopefully that began for her tomorrow when she started first grade.

And hopefully she would sleep without any of the nightmares that had plagued her since she was about three years old. There was nothing worse for a parent than to see their child suffer dreams that filled them with terror. Thankfully her nightmares were coming less and less often now.

He left the bedroom and went into the living room and sank down in his oversize easy chair. He was exhausted. Work on the farm was far more difficult, more strenuous than he'd thought it would be, but he was starting to learn some of the ins and outs and adjust to it.

His thoughts immediately went to his neighbor. He didn't even know her name, but he'd watched her several times ride across her pasture on horseback. It was definitely a sight to be seen.

She always looked as if she was one with her horse. Her long legs molded to the horse's flanks and her long blond hair flew out around her head as she galloped across the land.

He'd never seen a man around her place, although

it wasn't like he'd been watching her 24/7. She was just a mild distraction in his otherwise lonely life.

Maybe tomorrow, to celebrate the first day of school, he would take Emily into the café to eat. He'd had yet to go out and around in town.

It wouldn't hurt to head in and explore a little bit of the place they now called home, although he certainly wasn't looking for friends or any kind of a relationship for himself.

It would be too dangerous to get close to anyone. He had too many secrets…secrets that could mean a matter of life or death.

As long as Emily had lots of friends and plenty of happiness from now on, that's all he really cared about. He'd continue his life of loneliness to make sure she stayed safe and happy with him.

It was the price he'd pay for that fateful night of blood and death that had occurred a little under four years ago.

Chapter 2

"I can't believe I'm in here and doing this," Lizzy said the next afternoon. She and Bailey had shared a quick lunch at the café and now Lizzy sat in one of the chairs in the Sassy Nails Salon as Bailey painted her fingernails a pleasant shade of pink.

"I can't believe you didn't let me give you the fiery red nails that I know you could totally rock," Bailey replied. "So, what's on the menu for tonight? Chocolate cupcakes or maybe some of your famous chocolate chip cookies?" The two of them were the only ones in the salon at the moment.

"What makes you think anything like that would be on my menu for tonight?"

Bailey gave her a sly grin. "I know, because for

the first time in years, you're getting your nails done."

"Cookies," Lizzy confessed. "My double chocolate chip ones. I've never met a little girl who didn't like them."

"So, when exactly did you decide to do this?" Bailey asked as she finished up the last fingernail.

"I got into bed last night and started thinking about how remiss I've been as a member of the city council in not welcoming the new people to town."

"Is that your job on the city council…? Do we actually have some sort of welcome wagon?"

Lizzy laughed. "Definitely there's no official welcoming committee. We haven't had that many new people move to Millsville to warrant anything like that. I just realized that you were right, going over there and welcoming him and his daughter would be the real neighborly thing for me to do."

"And it doesn't hurt that I told you he was a real hottie," Bailey teased.

"I didn't even take that into consideration," Lizzy protested with a laugh. "You know, I'm the first one to admit I get lonely. But I'm not willing to fill the empty space in my life with just anyone."

"If you were willing to do that, you'd be with Barry Snyder right now. And remind me again what was wrong with him?" Bailey raised one of her pale eyebrows.

"He, uh, had that little throat-clearing issue," Lizzy replied. "He'd clear his voice after almost every sentence he spoke. I don't know if it was kind of a nervous habit or a real health issue, but it got on my nerves after a while."

"And what about Lynn Steran? He was crazy about you, and for a while there, I thought you seemed pretty crazy about him. And ultimately what was wrong with him?"

A faint blush warmed Lizzy's cheeks. "He wiggled his ears all the time. He thought it was charming. I thought it was charming and funny for a minute, and then I was over it, but he wouldn't stop."

"Admit it, Lizzy, you're way too picky when it comes to men. Are you sure you don't want me to paint a sparkly little heart or something else on your nails?"

"Don't push your luck," Lizzy replied with a laugh. "It's enough I got this much done."

Minutes later Lizzy walked down the sidewalk toward the feed store where she needed to order some supplies. Even though today was the first day of September and it was still warm, all the ranchers in the area were aware that winter was quickly approaching. And winters in this area of Kansas could be utterly brutal, with below freezing temperatures and lots and lots of snow.

"Hi, Lizzy. Where are you headed to this afternoon?" Fred Stanley stepped out of the alcove of the post office and fell into step with her.

Lizzy mentally stifled a groan and forced herself to smile at the old man. Fred was in his mid-eighties and had a reputation for being a lech with a nasty mouth. Even though he didn't walk that close to her, she could smell the sickening scent of his lime-based cologne. The man must positively bathe in it.

"Just going to the feed store and then home," she replied.

"Why don't you take me home with you, Lizzy? I could definitely tickle your fancy in ways you haven't even imagined," he said as he moved closer to her side.

Lizzy stopped in her tracks and turned to face him. "Fred Stanley, you know I'm not going to take you home with me and I thought you were warned by the police not to talk like that to the women in town."

"Talk like what? I was just telling you the truth." His watery blue eyes looked her up and down. "You're a mighty fine-looking woman, Lizzy. I can't help it that when I look at you Mr. Willie comes to life."

Lizzy gasped, and thankfully at that moment, Dallas Calloway approached the two of them. Dallas was a good-looking man with curly dark hair and gray eyes. He and Lizzy had gone out twice in the past but there had been no real sparks between them. They'd agreed to part ways and had remained good friends.

"Afternoon Lizzy… Fred," he said. "Fred, are you behaving yourself?" The head lawman in town eyed the old man firmly.

"'Course I am. I just stopped to say hello to Lizzy here, and now I'll just be on my way." He gave Lizzy a benign smile and then hurried on down the sidewalk.

"Thanks for the rescue," Lizzy said to Dallas. "He wanted to tell me how he could tickle my fancy."

Dallas frowned and shook his head. "I swear I don't know what to do with him. He's relatively harmless except for him running at the mouth about inappropriate things. If I locked him up every time he offended a woman, he'd be a permanent resident of the jail and he wouldn't learn his lesson anyway."

"Every town has to have one, right?" Lizzy said with a small laugh.

"I suppose," Dallas replied. "Are you okay?" he asked.

"Don't worry, Dallas. It will take far more than Fred's naughty mouthiness to make me not okay," she replied.

"I don't like to see you out here all alone," Dallas said as a new frown creased his forehead. "You know you fit the victim profile and I'm trying to keep you blond-haired, blue-eyed women off the streets or at least traveling with a male or in a group."

"I know, but you also know my situation, Dallas. I don't have a male in my life and my friends can't just drop everything for me. You know I don't come into town too often and when I do, I definitely watch my surroundings," she replied. "Any new clues yet?"

"Nothing. So far, this guy is like a damned ghost," Dallas said in obvious frustration. "The really upsetting part of this is I believe the killer lives right here. I believe it's somebody we probably all know, somebody we might smile at during the day."

"That's such a chilling thought," Lizzy said. "I just hope you find him before he makes the headlines again."

"That makes two of us. Now, go… Get your errands run and done and then get home safely," Dallas said.

"That's my plan. I'll see you later, Dallas," Lizzy replied and then hurried on down the sidewalk to the feed store. Once there, she ordered her supplies and then posted a help-wanted sign on the bulletin board that many people, especially the men, looked at. Bailey was right, it was time…past time to get some help for the ranch.

It was just after four by the time Lizzy got home. As she began to stir together the ingredients for her chocolate chip cookies, she thought about her brief conversation with Dallas.

The Scarecrow Killer and his murders had filled the headlines of the local newspaper for weeks. He'd finally fallen off the front page when somebody had tried to burn down the Sweet Tooth Bakery with the owner, Harper Brennan, inside. Thankfully Harper had been saved and the damage to the building was being fixed by her new husband, Sam Bravano, and his two brothers, who were all carpenters.

She shoved all thoughts of crime and killers out of her head as she spooned out the raw cookie dough onto two baking sheets and then popped them both into the oven. Within ten minutes the delicious scents of the baking cookies filled the air.

She'd decided she'd deliver them next door around six. Hopefully that would be after their dinner and before the little girl's bedtime.

Once the cookies were done, she ate a quick dinner of leftovers from the night before and then headed into her bedroom with the en suite bathroom.

Lizzy's mother had passed away from kidney disease when Lizzy was eleven years old. Rose Maxwell had been a soft-spoken, loving woman who Lizzy had mourned deeply. After her death, Lizzy's father had become a quiet, distant figure as he dealt with his own grief.

When Lizzy turned sixteen, her father had moved out of the master bedroom and had given it to Lizzy, telling her that every teenage girl needed her own bathroom. He'd let her redecorate everything in the bedroom to her own taste and she'd chosen decor in soft peaches and creams. Through the years she'd updated the bedroom but had stuck with the same color scheme.

She now went into the adjoining bathroom and started the shower, then undressed and threw her clothes into the nearby hamper. Minutes later as she stood beneath the warm spray of the water, she couldn't help but admire her newly pink nails.

It had been years since she'd had a real manicure. Had she decided to have one today because she was going to meet her new neighbor? She hated to admit that the answer was yes. As if he would care whether her nails were painted or not.

Bailey was right, Lizzy had been picky about the men she'd dated in the past. But she only wanted to get married once. If she didn't find her Mr. Perfect, then she was okay being all alone… At least that's what she told herself.

After drying off, she pulled on a clean pair of jeans and a white-and-pink-striped sleeveless blouse. She pulled her long hair into a high ponytail and then applied her makeup sparingly.

At precisely six o'clock she carried the cookies out to her pickup truck. As she started the truck, a wave of unexpected anxiety swept through her. Although Lizzy considered herself an extrovert, for some reason she felt unaccountably nervous about introducing herself to the man next door. Maybe it was because he'd moved in there over two months ago and she should have introduced herself long before now. Or perhaps it was because Bailey had said he was a hottie.

She drove down the road and turned onto the next-door property. The house was much like her own, a rambling ranch style. Where her house was painted a dark gray, this place was painted a dark brown with rust-colored shutters. A large barn sat behind the house, along with a small stable and other outbuildings.

On the left side of the house was a sizable cornfield. The green stalks were tall and it wouldn't be long before harvesting time. To the right of the house was the pasture that separated her property from his.

The previous owners had been an old couple who had told her over three months ago that they were ready to sell and retire from ranch life. It seemed like one minute they'd been there, and the next minute, they'd been gone and the new neighbor had taken over lock, stock and barrel.

She pulled up toward the front door and then parked. She grabbed the tin full of the cookies and got out of the truck. Once again, a wave of nervous energy shot through her.

Maybe he'd be a nice man who would make a pleasant neighbor. In this farming community, neighbors were like family. Or it was possible he was a cranky man who wanted to be left all alone. Either way, she'd know in minutes.

Clint sat in his chair, dividing his attention between a crime drama show on television and Emily playing with a baby doll on the sofa.

"Look, Daddy, I wrapped Annie in her nice pink blankie," she said.

"She looks very comfortable," he replied with a smile.

"She's gonna take a nap. I don't have to take naps anymore, right, Daddy?"

"That's right. You don't have to take naps anymore because you're a big girl."

"I'm a big girl and I go to first grade now," Emily said with a happy smile of her own.

The first day of school for Emily had been a rousing success. She'd come home happy and chatting about all the new friends she'd made and how much she loved her teacher, Mrs. Barlow.

He'd intended to take her into the café for dinner to celebrate, but she'd told him she wanted his hot dogs and baked beans for dinner that night, so they'd stayed at home to eat.

"I got to go get baby Becky. I think she needs a nap, too." Emily ran back to her bedroom. She returned a moment later with the second baby doll in her arms.

A knock shot Clint up and out of his chair. His first thought was to go grab his gun in his bedroom before opening the door.

"Daddy… Daddy…somebody is here." Emily danced around the foyer with excitement.

Instead of running to his bedroom to get his gun, Clint did the reasonable thing and looked out the peephole. Her. Even though he hadn't seen her features up close before, he instantly recognized the woman as his neighbor.

He opened the door and she immediately smiled at him. Oh…she was far prettier than he'd imagined. Her eyes were a beautiful blue with long dark lashes. Her features were perfect and delicate and he instantly felt a jolt of unexpected physical attraction that absolutely surprised him.

"Hi," she said. "I'm Lizzy Maxwell. I, uh, live next door and I thought I'd just come over here and welcome you and your daughter to the area."

"Please…come in." He opened the screen door to

allow her into the foyer. As she swept past him, he caught the scents of sweet flowers and an underlying spice that was instantly pleasing.

"Hi, my name is Emily," his daughter said and smiled her prettiest smile at the female stranger.

"Hello, Emily. It's so nice to meet you." Lizzy leaned down slightly to put herself on Emily's level. "I hope you like chocolate chip cookies because I brought you some."

Emily clapped her hands together. "I love chocolate chip cookies. They're my very favorite."

"What do you say, Emily?" Clint asked.

"Thank you," Emily replied.

Lizzy straightened. "How about I give these to your daddy and he can tell you when you can have one." Lizzy held out the cookie tin to Clint.

"Thank you, that's very kind of you. Please, come in and have a seat," he said and gestured her toward the family room.

"Well, maybe just for a few minutes," she replied.

He couldn't help but notice as he followed behind her that her jeans hugged her long legs and pert derriere perfectly. He pointed her toward the sofa. "Can I get you something to drink? Maybe a soda or a cup of coffee?"

"No, thanks. I'm fine." She sat on the sofa and Emily immediately curled up right next to her. Clint sat in the overstuffed chair facing the sofa.

"You have pink fingernails like me," Emily said,

obviously delighted by the similarity as she displayed her little nails to Lizzy. "My daddy painted mine."

"That was very nice of him and they look very pretty," Lizzy replied with a quick smile at Clint.

"Daddy fixes my hair, too. Daddy, tomorrow I want to wear a ponytail like hers," she said.

"I'll see what I can do, bug," he replied. There were mornings when he just had trouble getting a brush through Emily's thick, long blond hair.

Emily sidled even closer to Lizzy. "Are you a mommy?" she asked. Clint was appalled. Lizzy shot him a quick look of surprise and then she looked back at his daughter.

"No, sweetie, I'm not a mommy."

"Do you want to be one?" Emily asked.

"Uh, Emily, why don't you go play in your room for a little while so I can have some grown-up time with Ms. Maxwell," Clint said before Lizzy could answer.

Emily slid off the sofa with obvious reluctance. "But can I have a cookie later?"

"Yes, you can have a cookie before bedtime," Clint replied. "And again, what do you say to Ms. Maxwell?"

"Thank you for the cookies. Maybe sometime you could come and play with me."

"Now, off you go," Clint said hurriedly.

He waited until Emily disappeared into her bedroom and then he smiled apologetically at Lizzy. "Sorry about that."

"Please don't apologize. She's absolutely charming," Lizzy replied.

"Thanks, I think so, but I'm also a bit partial," Clint replied. "And I didn't even properly introduce myself. I'm Clint Kincaid."

"Nice to meet you, Clint Kincaid." Lizzy smiled once again.

She had a beautiful smile. It not only curved her slightly plump lips upward, but it also sparked in her eyes and warmed her beautiful features.

"So, where do you come from, Clint?" she asked.

Clint's muscles all tensed. It was time to start the lies, and although he hated having to tell them, it was imperative that he did. Hopefully he wouldn't screw things up. "California...the Los Angeles area."

"Oh wow, so what brought you all the way from California to Millsville, Kansas?" She leaned forward slightly, making him feel as if she was totally engaged in the conversation. It was an attractive trait.

"I know it sounds kind of ridiculous, but I had always dreamed about being a cowboy and farmer and living on a ranch in the Midwest. When I got divorced a couple of years ago, I decided it was time to quit my job in corporate America and work toward making my dream come true. I had an agent looking for properties for me and he ran across this one for sale. I made an offer that was accepted, then I tied up my life in California and here we are."

Had he said too much? Too little? Had it all sounded believable? She was the first person he'd told these lies to. It was important that everyone believed his cover story.

"Then welcome to your dream," she replied.

He immediately relaxed and laughed. "I'm finding my dream a little more difficult than I initially thought. I'll admit that I definitely had a romanticized view of farming and ranching."

"It is a lot of hard work," she replied. "If you ever have any questions about anything, I'm right next door and I'd be glad to help you out in any way I can."

"Thanks, I really appreciate that," he replied.

"That's one thing you'll find out about Millsville. The town is filled with a lot of wonderful people and we're generally a loving, caring community."

"Except for a serial killer who is on the loose. I've been reading the headlines for the last couple of months," he said.

A frown etched across her forehead, not taking anything away from her attractiveness. "This has never happened before in our town and I know the entire police department is working overtime to solve the crimes. I'm just hoping the killer is caught quickly so we can all finally relax once again."

He knew from reading the news reports that the last two victims had been blonde women with blue eyes, just like Lizzy. "I don't know if you live alone or not, but if you ever need any help, remember I'm just here next door."

"I am alone and I appreciate it. Maybe we should exchange phone numbers," she suggested.

"That's a great idea." He picked up his phone from the end table next to him as she dug into her purse and then pulled hers out. It took them only a few moments to trade information and then she stood.

"I should probably get out of here now. I'm sure you have lots of things to attend to before a little girl's bedtime."

As if she'd heard the vague reference to her, Emily came running back into the room as Clint stood. He was reluctant to say goodbye to Lizzy. It had been nice to have her company if only for a little while.

Emily grabbed hold of Lizzy's hand as they all walked to the front door. "Will you come over again?" she asked. "You could play with my baby dolls. I'll share with you."

"Thank you, Emily. That's very sweet of you," Lizzy replied.

"So, will you come over again?" Emily pressed.

"I'm sure Ms. Maxwell is busy with all her own work," Clint said.

"But I'll see you again, Emily. And please call me Lizzy," she said.

"Ms. Lizzy," Clint said to his daughter.

Clint opened the door and Emily dropped Lizzy's hand. "Thank you again for the cookies and for coming over," Clint said. "It's been a real pleasure."

Lizzy offered him another one of her gorgeous smiles. "Now we're truly neighbors and not strangers."

"I like that," Clint replied with a smile of his own. "Good night, Lizzy."

"'Night, Ms. Lizzy," Emily said.

"Good night," she replied.

He stepped out on the porch to watch her get into her truck. He remained there until her taillights were visible as she pulled into her own place next door.

"Guess what time it is," he said to Emily once he was back inside with the door locked.

"Cookie time?" she asked tentatively.

He scooped her up in his arms, loving the sound of her giggles. "That's right, it's cookie time." He grabbed the tin from the end table where he'd placed it when Lizzy had given it to him.

He carried Emily into the kitchen and deposited her on a chair at the table. He then opened the tin and the scent of chocolate and goodness radiated upward.

"How about a glass of milk and two cookies and then straight into the bathtub?" he said.

"'Kay," she agreed happily.

The cookies were delicious and after the two of them had their treats, it was time for Emily to take her bath and get ready for bed.

About forty-five minutes later Clint sat next to her bed. "I like Ms. Lizzy. Did you like her, Daddy?" Emily asked.

"She seems like a very nice lady," he replied.

"I think she would make a good mommy," Emily said.

"Honey, Lizzy isn't going to be your mommy. She's

just our neighbor." He leaned forward and kissed her on the forehead. "Now, go to sleep so you're ready for school tomorrow."

With his daughter in bed, Clint returned to his chair in the living room with Lizzy Maxwell still on his mind. He'd definitely been physically drawn to her.

It hadn't just been about her long legs and the full breasts that had pressed against her blouse. It had also been about her wide, open smiles and the warm spark in her beautiful eyes.

He wondered if he was at a place where he'd be drawn to any woman who gave him the time of day. Was he so lonely that he would have enjoyed just anyone's company?

Somehow he didn't think so. His attraction was Lizzy Maxell specific. He wished she would have stayed longer. It had been nice to have a conversation with another adult. He definitely would have enjoyed getting to know her a little better.

She'd said she lived alone. Did that mean she wasn't dating anyone? Was she available to pursue a relationship with? He mentally shook himself.

What was wrong with him? It didn't matter whether she was available or not. He couldn't risk having a relationship with anyone. Lizzy had believed his initial lies tonight, but by getting closer to her, it was possible he'd say something or do something he shouldn't.

Besides, it wouldn't be fair for him to get involved with anyone considering his entire life now was based on nothing more than lies.

Chapter 3

Clint Kincaid was positively drop-dead gorgeous. Lizzy parked and went back into her home, her thoughts on the man she had just left. Bailey had definitely been so right. The man was a total hottie and exactly Lizzy's type.

She went into the living room and sank down on the sofa. Her head instantly filled with a vision of her neighbor. His hair was thick, black and slightly shaggy, and his eyes were a piercing blue that she'd instantly found half-mesmerizing. His features were bold and handsomely defined.

Not only that, but his shoulders were broad, his waist was slim and his legs were long. "Oh, be still my heart," she now said with a small laugh at herself.

Emily seemed like a real sweetheart, and something about the little girl asking her if she was a mommy had touched Lizzy's heart. She wondered where Emily's mommy was. Why wasn't she in Emily's life? Or maybe she was. Lizzy certainly didn't know anything about Clint's situation with his former wife and their child.

It had been a long time since a man had really attracted Lizzy and she was definitely attracted to her new neighbor. It probably hadn't been particularly wise to tell a virtual stranger that she lived here alone, but she'd wanted Clint to know she was available, and she also knew he wasn't the Scarecrow Killer.

Besides, she was confident that Dallas would have checked out the new guy in town for the timing of when the murders had occurred and where Clint had been on those occasions.

She'd made the first move by going over there and introducing herself to him and now the ball was in his court. She desperately hoped he would take the next step.

The following day she was unsurprised when Bailey showed up just after breakfast time. It was Wednesday and the nail shop was closed on Sundays and Wednesdays.

"Somehow I knew I'd see you first thing this morning," Lizzy said as she opened the door to her best friend.

"Give me coffee and then I want to hear all the

juicy details about Operation Cookie," Bailey replied.

Lizzy laughed as she led Bailey into the kitchen. She poured them each a cup of coffee and then she joined her friend at the table.

"Now, tell me all," Bailey demanded.

"I delivered some cookies next door last night and that's it," Lizzy said airily. "It was no big deal."

"Oh no, you don't, girlfriend. I need each and every single detail," Bailey replied.

Lizzy took a sip of her coffee and then leaned forward. "Oh, Bailey, you were so right. He's an absolute hunk," she said as she put her cup back down.

"I knew you'd think so. Physically he's definitely the type you're always drawn to."

"He is. I love a black-haired, blue-eyed kind of guy," Lizzy replied.

"So, what was he like?"

"He was nice…very nice and his daughter is a real cutie. He's from California and this is the first time he's trying his hand at ranching and farming. Of course, I told him he was welcome to call me with any questions or concerns he might have."

"Of course you did," Bailey said with a grin. She took a drink of her coffee and then lowered the cup. "Sounds like somebody might have a little crush," she added with a raised brow.

"I'll admit it, I do have a little crush," Lizzy replied. "We exchanged phone numbers so we'll see if he calls me."

"Did he indicate any interest in you?"

Lizzy sighed. "I don't know... It was hard to tell. I mean, he was very friendly, but I'm sure he would have been nice to anyone who showed up on his doorstep with homemade cookies for his daughter."

"I guess time will tell if he's interested in you or not," Bailey replied.

Time did tell. The next week flew by without a phone call from Clint. Lizzy couldn't help but be disappointed about it. Still, she told herself that just because Clint was her type, that didn't mean that she was his.

Thursday evening, she was once again seated at the long table in city hall for another city council meeting. There was a total of five people on the council and Mayor Buddy Lyons made six, although he didn't vote on matters. He was simply there to facilitate the meeting.

Letta Lee sat next to her good friend and sycophant, Mabel Tredway. Both of the older women glared at Lizzy. Butch Randolf and Paul Crawford made up the other two members of the council. Both of them were middle-aged farmers.

"So, what do we have to do to get this damned budget passed?" Butch asked and looked directly at Lizzy. He was a big bald man with dark eyes that now flashed with anger.

"As far as I'm concerned, we need to modify some of the numbers," Lizzy replied calmly. "We're a small town with limited tax revenues and the budget as it stands is just too big. It will be an unnecessary burden on every single taxpayer in town, and many of them just can't afford that right now."

"Well, I need every dime of what I proposed for the women's gardening club," Letta Lee replied haughtily. "The club is vital to the health and well-being of all the women in town."

As far as Lizzy was concerned the gardening club was Letta Lee's very own little clique, a clique who froze out members who didn't fit the Letta Lee narrative of worshiping her.

"And I'm not budging on what I proposed for the roads," Butch replied. "There's a lot of potholes out there that need to be fixed before winter comes."

"Surely we could get some volunteers to help with the roadwork, and I don't understand why the gardening club can't do some events, like bake sales or garage sales or whatever, to help them with their financial needs," Lizzy replied.

"We don't do bake sales," Letta replied thinly. "We certainly don't do garage sales. We don't do anything like that."

"That's right," Mabel echoed her friend.

"So, what do we need to do to get you to vote yes to the budget?" Paul asked Lizzy.

"You all know what you need to do. Cut the budget," Lizzy replied patiently. "We all know that farmers in the area are struggling right now. Elijah Simpson and his food bank are helping more people than ever before. If I'm a part of passing this astronomical budget that's going to put the strain on the very back of the community, I wouldn't be able to sleep nights."

"Dammit, Lizzy, just vote yes so we can get this done and over with," Butch said angrily. "I got more important things to do than to keep coming to these meetings where you're being a stubborn bitch."

Lizzy drew in a shocked breath.

"Whoa, there's no need to curse at each other," Buddy said. "That's not necessary. What I suggest now is we all go home and take a second look at things. Let's figure out a way to cut what we can and then meet back here again in two weeks."

Lizzy didn't stick around to chitchat after the meeting. She beelined for the door and then left the building, knowing that the others were ticked off at her. But she couldn't vote against her conscience and she definitely wouldn't be bullied into doing so. Butch could call her all kinds of nasty names, but that wasn't going to sway her.

Times had gotten more difficult for everyone. Prices for necessities were rising and many people were financially struggling like they never had before. They didn't need to be burdened by more taxes to pay for the garden club to have tea and crumpets every time they met.

She got into her truck to head home. She passed the three giant grain silos that served the town and provided the only cityscape the small town had. Once she left the city limits, she glanced in her rearview mirror and saw another truck in the distance coming up on her fast.

Was that Butch's pickup? He lived on a ranch on the other side of town. What would he be doing out here? Was it possible he was following her now to somehow bully her some more? She knew the man had a hair-trigger temper. She'd seen it on display at meetings before.

She tightened her hands on the steering wheel as the truck came closer and closer to her back end. It was too dark to tell the color of the vehicle. Half the farmers in Millsville drove black or dark blue pickups.

They were on a narrow road with no lighting, and her heart accelerated as the truck came closer and closer...so close to her that she could no longer see his headlights.

She tensed and prepared to be rear-ended. At this speed, even if he just tapped her bumper, it could mean a complete disaster. Her breath whooshed out of her as the truck shot around her and continued on its way.

Knowing that Butch was angry with her and that there was a serial killer somewhere out there, she was obviously on edge more than usual.

It was with a sigh of relief when she finally walked through her front door. She locked it behind her and then checked her watch. It was a few minutes after eight and she had yet to eat dinner.

She made herself a ham-and-cheese sandwich and

added a handful of potato chips to the plate. She got back up to grab a sofa from the fridge and then she sank down at the table.

She was halfway through with her sandwich when her phone rang. The caller ID came up as anonymous. She frowned and answered.

"Bitch." The word exploded over the line.

"Who is this?" she asked, shocked by the male voice she didn't recognize.

Click. The caller hung up.

The phone rang again and once again the ID was anonymous. She answered. "You are a damned bitch," the same caller said and then once again hung up.

The phone rang for a third time and Lizzy grabbed it up. "I got the message, I'm a bitch, now stop calling me."

There was a long pause. "Lizzy, uh, it's Clint, uh, your neighbor."

Lordy, she was absolutely mortified. "Oh…hi, Clint."

"Is everything all right?" His deep, smooth voice seemed to caress the rough edges that the previous two calls had created.

"Everything is fine, I just had a couple of nasty phone calls, but I'm okay."

"I'm sorry to hear that," he replied. "Are you sure you're okay?"

"I'm positive."

"Well, the reason for my call is I was wondering

if you'd like to have dinner tomorrow night with me and Emily at the café."

"Oh, that would be very nice," she replied as her heart did a little dance of joy. "I'd love to."

"Great. How about we pick you up around five thirty?"

"That sounds fine. I'll be ready."

Once they said their goodbyes, Lizzy fist-pumped the air with excitement and immediately called Bailey. "Guess who just called me and ask me to have dinner at the café tomorrow night with him and his daughter?"

"Gee, let me take a wild guess... Your neighbor?"

"That's right," Lizzy replied. "Oh Bailey, I'm so excited."

"What are you going to wear? Please don't wear that blue-striped jumpsuit that bunches up in your belly every time you sit down. It makes you look pregnant."

Lizzy laughed. "Don't worry, that blue jumpsuit hit the donation bag a long time ago. I was actually thinking about wearing my pink-and-white sundress if the weather stays warm enough."

"That's good, you look really cute in that," Bailey replied. "I hope you have a good time, but I figure if you go out with him two or three times, you'll eventually find something wrong with him."

"I hope not," Lizzy replied fervently. "I'm definitely interested in him, but we might go out tomorrow night and he'll realize he's not that into me. Or I might realize he's just not the one for me."

"That's possible, too. Only time will tell," Bailey said.

The hours moved agonizingly slow through the next day as Lizzy took care of all the daily chores. But finally, it was nearly time for Clint and Emily to pick Lizzy up for the dinner out.

She now stood in front of the bathroom mirror to check herself out. She knew the light pink-and-white sundress looked nice on her, and although she rarely wore makeup, tonight her cheeks held a faint hue of blush and her lashes were lengthened and darkened by mascara.

She spritzed on her favorite perfume and then went into the living room to wait for their arrival. Nerves bounced and jumped in the pit of her stomach as she contemplated the evening to come.

Despite how handsome Clint was and in spite of how nice he had been to her; she knew it was quite possible there would be no real sparks between them. He might just be a kind, great-looking guy and a good neighbor, but nothing more to Lizzy. Still, he had to feel some sort of attraction to her, because he'd invited her out.

She'd know exactly what he was going to be to her by the end of the evening. Once again, her nerves jumped in the pit of her stomach as she thought about spending the evening with the very hot Clint and the cute little Emily.

* * *

After Lizzy's initial visit, Clint had told himself she would remain his neighbor and nothing more. There was no question that he'd been very attracted to her, but he knew to have any kind of a real relationship with her would be a mistake.

However, Emily had other ideas. Each evening she asked him when they were going to see Ms. Lizzy again. There was no question he would like to see her again, so finally he'd broken down and called her about having dinner with them. A meal with his daughter present should be fairly benign. It was something neighbors might do together.

He now pulled up in front of Lizzy's house and he was surprised at the nervous energy that shot through his veins. After everything that had happened in his life, he was surprised anything could make him nervous anymore.

He parked and turned to Emily, who was strapped in her car seat in the back. "You stay here and I'll be right back with Ms. Lizzy," he told her.

"Hurry, Daddy," she replied. "I can't wait to see Ms. Lizzy again."

He left the car and walked the few steps to the front door. Her house was painted an attractive gray with black accents and it appeared that it probably had the same floor plan as his.

He knocked and she answered almost immediately. She looked even prettier than he remembered.

The pink-and-white dress cinched her slender waist and showcased her full breasts.

Her hair was shiny and loose to just beneath her shoulders and his fingers immediately itched to play in the long golden strands. She carried a purse that perfectly matched the pink in her dress, making her appear completely pulled together.

"Hi, Clint," she greeted him with a smile that immediately shot a wave of warmth to the pit of his stomach.

"Evening, Lizzy. You look really nice."

"Thank you. You look really nice, too."

He had chosen a pair of navy slacks and a light blue polo shirt for the evening. "Thanks, are you all ready to go?"

"I'm ready." She stepped out on the porch and closed her door behind her. He immediately smelled her, that floral-and-spice mixture he found extremely pleasant.

"I'd better warn you Emily has been asking about you all week and she is really excited to see you again," he said as he walked her to the passenger side of his truck.

"That's so sweet and I'm looking forward to spending more time with her. She seems like a real delight."

He opened the passenger door and immediately Emily squealed with excitement. "Ms. Lizzy... Ms. Lizzy, I'm so happy to see you."

Lizzy laughed. "And I'm so happy to see you

again." Lizzy slid into the seat and Clint closed the door and then hurried around to the driver's side.

When he got in behind the wheel, Emily was telling Lizzy all about her first week of school. "And I got smiley faces on all my papers and I made a lot of new friends and I love school and my teacher."

"That's wonderful, Emily," Lizzy replied. "And have you thought about what you're going to order for dinner tonight?"

"Ice cream," Emily replied immediately.

"I think you might need to eat something else before the ice cream," Clint said. "Now, let me visit with Ms. Lizzy for a few minutes."

"'Kay," Emily replied and focused her attention on the kids' tablet he'd bought her a month ago.

Clint shot a grin at Lizzy. "Hi."

She laughed. He loved the sound. Her laughter was so musical and infectious. "Hi, yourself," she replied.

"This will be our first visit to the café. So, what should I expect?" he asked as he pulled out of her drive and onto the road that would take them into town.

"A very pleasant atmosphere and good food," she replied.

"Have you brought your appetite this evening?" he asked.

"Definitely," she replied. "And I have to warn you I'm not one of those women who order a house salad and then pick at it and say I'm good. I like food and I love to eat."

He laughed. "Good, I'm glad. I enjoy food and it's nice to be with somebody else who enjoys it as well. Do you have a favorite dish at the café?"

"Ice cream," Emily quipped from the back seat. Both Clint and Lizzy laughed.

"Actually, I don't have a specific favorite. Everything I've ever ordered there has been good," Lizzy said.

"Then, I'm really looking forward to this."

A silence filled the truck…a silence that grew slightly uncomfortable as it lingered. Thankfully before it got too awkward, he reached the café.

"Looks like it's a full house," he said as he circled the parking lot in the back, looking for an empty space. He'd already looked for one in front of the café, but there had been no free places.

"Friday nights and Sunday afternoons are the busiest times at the café. They are peak gossip times in Millsville," Lizzy replied with a small laugh. "I probably should have warned you."

"A little gossip doesn't bother me," he replied. He'd assumed people might speculate and talk when he brought Lizzy to the café. That didn't mean anyone was going to do a deep dive into his background.

He finally found an empty parking space and pulled in. It took them only minutes to get out of the truck and then Emily grabbed his hand and Lizzy's, and together the three of them walked toward the entrance.

For just a moment his heart clenched with thoughts

of what might have been had it not been for that terrible, bloody night so long ago. It would have been a different woman walking with him and Emily. He shoved aside all thoughts of that and instead focused on the here and now.

They entered the café and Clint looked around with interest. The walls were painted with images that fit the landscape where he now lived. One wall had golden haystacks and bright red roosters, another depicted a cornfield with three big silos, and the final wall was a patchwork of farmland in browns, golds and greens.

The air was redolent with the scents of frying burgers and baked bread, of simmering vegetables and other appetizing smells. The place was buzzing with conversations and the clink of silverware. A hostess greeted them and took them to an empty booth toward the back of the establishment.

She left them with a promise to return with a booster seat. Emily was small for her age and people always assumed she was younger than her years. Still, a booster seat usually made things easier for her.

"You won't find a place like this anywhere in New York," he said and then mentally kicked himself. Damn. He'd just slipped up. "Or in California," he quickly added.

"Oh, you've been to New York?" Lizzy asked, her beautiful blue eyes gazing at him curiously from across the table.

"I've visited there a couple of times," he replied. He had to keep it together and adhere to his new life story. He was now a man from California and not from New York.

"Have you visited other places?" she asked.

Her question let him know he was still safe. "I spent a weekend in Las Vegas and a week in the Bahamas, but those trips were all pre-Emily."

"Daddy, I want ice cream," Emily said.

"You can have ice cream for dessert, but you have to eat something else first," he said to his daughter.

At that moment the waitress returned with the booster seat and then she took their orders. Lizzy ordered the country fried steak platter, he asked for the fried chicken, and he got chicken fingers and mac and cheese for Emily. The waitress then gave Emily a paper to color and a small pack of crayons, which immediately got her busy.

Once the waitress had delivered their drinks, they settled in to wait for their food. "What about you?" he asked Lizzy, picking up on the conversation they'd previously been having. "Have you ever done any traveling?"

"Unfortunately, no. I've never had the time or the money. Since you're new to the ranching and farming business, I'll tell you a little secret about them. They are jealous mistresses that suck up all your time, your money and your energy."

"And yet you love it," he observed.

She laughed. "I do. Of course, it's all I've ever

known, but I can't imagine doing anything else in the world."

Once their food was delivered, their conversation continued as they got to know each other a little better. He was pleased to discover that they both had similar tastes in television shows and enjoyed the same kind of music.

Several people stopped by their booth to say hello to Lizzy. She introduced each of them to Clint and he knew by the end of the evening his head would be spinning with all the new names and faces. Still, it was evident that Lizzy was not only well-liked in her own town but also highly respected.

The conversation over dinner continued to be light and easy and she was very sweet with Emily, taking the time to talk to her. Lizzy looked so pretty. He had to admit that something about her shot a bit of tension through him, and it definitely wasn't an unpleasant tension.

"How about some dessert and coffee?" he asked once their empty plates were taken away. He wasn't ready to call it a night yet.

"Ice cream," Emily exclaimed.

"That sounds good to me," Lizzy said. "I wouldn't mind some ice cream with a cup of coffee."

"All I need to know is what flavor of ice cream you want," Clint replied.

"Chocolate," the two females replied at the same time, and then they both laughed.

"Oh, I love you, Ms. Lizzy," Emily said with an adoring look at Lizzy.

"And I think you're the sweetest, best-behaved and most beautiful little girl that I've ever met," Lizzy replied. Clint smiled at his daughter.

He was so proud of her and how she was behaving. But he shouldn't be surprised. Emily was almost always a well-behaved child. Still, it was obvious Emily was developing a strong hero worship for the new neighbor.

"Thank you," Emily said with her most charming smile. "Maybe you could come home with us tonight and you could tuck me into bed and then stay the night so I could see you first thing in the morning when I wake up. Daddy makes really good breakfasts."

Clint looked at his daughter in shocked surprise and then looked at Lizzy. Lizzy smiled warmly at Emily. "I'm so sorry, Emily, but I can't do that tonight, but maybe you and I could plan a play date together."

Emily clapped her hands together. "Yes, yes," she replied. "A play date. When? Soon, right?"

"Your daddy and I will have to make plans," Lizzy said. "I promise it will be soon."

Clint ordered ice cream for the two and then got a piece of banana cream pie for himself. Over dessert they chatted about her work on the city council and her volunteering for the local food bank. He then talked to her about a problem he had, a problem that he'd realized over the last couple of weeks or so.

"I need to find a housekeeper and babysitter," he said. "Somebody who could take Emily to school in the mornings and then come back to stay with Emily right after school. Maybe she could work some on the weekends so I can get more time out in the fields. Do you happen to know anybody who is completely trustworthy?"

"Actually, I do know somebody. Her name is Rosa Mendoza and she is a lovely older woman who is a widow and just recently stopped working for the Welch family because those kids are old enough the family didn't need her anymore. I'd be happy to text you her number tomorrow."

"Thanks. That would be great. Do you know if she happens to cook?" he asked.

"You don't?" she said in surprise.

"I do okay with easy things, but there are nights I get hungry for a nice meatloaf or maybe chicken that doesn't come from a box."

"Oh, you poor man…eating chicken from a box," Lizzy replied with her eyes twinkling teasingly. "Maybe you and Emily would like to come over to my place on Sunday around one for a meal of chicken and dumplings…chicken that definitely doesn't come out of a box."

"That would be amazing," he replied. "We would love to come." He was delighted, not just by the anticipation of a good meal, but rather by the fact she apparently wanted to see him again. "You'll need to let me know what we can bring."

"Just bring yourselves, I'll take care of the rest," she replied.

Unfortunately, much as he hated it, it was time to bring this evening to an end. Their desserts had been eaten and once he paid the check, they all left the café.

"I ate too much," Lizzy said as they walked toward his truck in the parking lot.

"Me, too," Emily said and grabbed hold of Lizzy's hand. "I ate too much just like you, Ms. Lizzy."

Clint was grateful that Lizzy didn't seem to mind. In fact, she had been patient and so caring with his daughter throughout the evening. It had definitely warmed his heart.

Maybe that's what drew him to her, the fact that she was very kind to Emily. However, he knew it was far more than that.

Everything he learned about her made the adrenaline inside him surge stronger.

He found her physically sexy as hell, and she reminded him that it had been a very long time since he'd been with a woman. Could he really pursue a relationship with her and keep his secrets safe?

Only time would tell.

He stood behind a large tree on her property, making sure he was hidden as the truck pulled in and parked near the front door. He watched as the two adults got out and headed for the door.

Immediately he could tell they were into each other. Their body language screamed it as they paused at her door. He leaned into her and then she leaned toward him. It was definitely a dance of a budding romance.

Perfect. She was absolutely perfect with her long blond hair and he just knew her eyes would be a sparkling blue. She was just like the last one.

Oh yes, it was going to be so much fun. This was really perfect. All he had to do was watch and learn and be patient and then he'd have his perfect revenge.

Chapter 4

Along with her usual morning chores outside on Sunday, Lizzy also gave her house a good cleaning in anticipation of having guests at one o'clock. She'd firmed up the time the day before when she had called him with Rosa Mendoza's contact information.

By noon the house smelled of the chicken and dumplings that were warming in a pot on the stovetop and an underlying scent of lemon furniture polish. There was also the aroma of apples and cinnamon as she'd made an apple pie for dessert.

The kitchen table was set with her mother's china, which her father had kept for her after her mother's death. Lizzy was also serving a cold cranberry salad with celery and pecans, sweet corn and homemade rolls.

Once everything was done, she walked into the living room to make sure she hadn't missed cleaning anything. After her father's death, she'd finally gotten rid of the green corduroy sofa and chair that had been in the room for as long as she could remember.

She'd replaced them with a beige, contemporary-style set. On the sofa she had pillows in bright turquoise and yellow. She'd kept the bookshelves that held her father's collection of painted cows. The little farm animals were painted in various colors and with specific themes. Her father had spent a lot of time going to garage sales and hitting thrift stores in search of the little cows.

He'd never invited her to go with him on one of his expeditions in hunt of the cows. For a moment as she looked at them, a wave of grief swept through her. Despite the fact that she'd nursed her father until his death, she'd never really felt her father's love for her. He held his grief over his wife's death up like a barrier to keep others out, including his only daughter.

Maybe her own grief over that was why she wanted to get married and make a family of her own so desperately…because her first family had been torn apart by a woman's death and a man's anguish. She would love to build the family she'd never had.

In the family she dreamed of, love was on the table every single day. Not necessarily lovemaking, but the little things, like a quick, unexpected kiss in the middle of the morning or a loving pat on the back or a gentle squeeze of the shoulder. It also might be a smoldering or affectionate gaze across the dinner table. She just believed it was important to share affirmations of love each single day.

She knew she was fantasizing a lot, but she truly believed that when she found the right man, her fantasies would come true. But first she wanted to fall madly and crazy in love with some wonderful man.

With that thought in mind she hurried on to her bedroom to change her clothes and put on a little makeup. It was after twelve thirty when she went back into the kitchen clad in a clean pair of jeans, a pink, summery blouse and with her eyelashes enhanced by mascara.

She was ridiculously nervous to see Clint again. She'd spoken to him briefly on the phone yesterday to give him Rosa Mendoza's phone number and to firm up the time for today.

However, talking to him on the phone wasn't as nerve-racking as seeing him in person again. There was no question she liked him and she wanted him to like her, too. Emily was a cute little loving bonus in the situation.

She double-checked that the dumplings weren't getting soggy and then placed the butter dish and the cranberry salad on the table. The burgundy salad looked pretty against the delicate flowers on the china, which were the same color.

The house was clean, the table looked pretty, and with a final stir to the chicken and dumplings and the saucepan full of corn, she then went back into the living room to await her guests.

She sank down on the sofa and drew several deep breaths in an effort to calm her nerves. She had really enjoyed having dinner out with him and Emily. Each and every thing she'd learned about him had only made her more interested in him.

There was no question that she was physically drawn to him. His nearness caused a breathless excitement deep inside her. She'd half hoped he might kiss her goodbye that night, but he hadn't.

She couldn't be upset about it, since his daughter had been in the truck, awaiting his return. What surprised her was that she'd wanted him to kiss her in the first place. After all, it had only been their first date so to speak.

It was exactly one o'clock when she heard the crunch of gravel that led up to her driveway. A quick glance out the window showed her Clint's truck pulling up.

She watched them get out. Clint looked tall and handsome in a pair of jeans and a white short-sleeved shirt that exposed his nice biceps. Emily looked like a little doll in a pink sundress and with her long hair pulled up into pigtails. He reached in to grab something out of the passenger seat and then they moved up the walkway.

Lizzy went to the front door and opened it. "Hi, neighbors," she said.

Clint offered her a smile that instantly heated her

blood. At the same time, Emily squealed with excitement. "We match, Ms. Lizzy," she exclaimed. "We're both pink."

"We are, indeed," Lizzy replied with a laugh.

"I brought some crumb cakes from the bakery for dessert," he said and held out the bakery box.

"Thank you, but that wasn't necessary," she replied.

She ushered the two into the living room. "The meal is ready. I thought we could eat first and then relax and visit more after we're done."

"Sounds like a good plan to me," he replied.

"Great. Just follow me. I set up in the kitchen instead of the dining room. It's a little friendlier than the more formal setting in the other room." She set the bakery box on the counter next to her apple pie.

"The table looks really nice and something smells absolutely delicious," he said as they followed her into the kitchen.

"Thanks," she replied. He definitely smelled delicious. His cologne was fresh and clean-smelling. She'd noticed it on Friday night when they'd gone out. It was a scent that stirred her in a very good way.

"Feel free to sit anywhere," she said. The table was round, so there was no head of the table to deal with. She frowned. "Unfortunately, I don't have a booster seat."

"Actually, I have one in the car. It just felt weird to bring it in when we first arrived," he confessed. "I guess I didn't want you to think we were moving in on you."

She laughed. "Go get the booster seat and Emily and I will be here when you get back."

"On my way," he said and then disappeared from the kitchen.

"Emily, would you like to help me with something?" Lizzy asked the little girl.

"Yes, yes, I'll help you, Ms. Lizzy," she replied eagerly. "I like to help."

"Great, I have these rolls and they need to all be placed in this basket." Lizzy placed the cooled baking sheet with the rolls on the table and then handed her a basket with a checkered cloth napkin in the bottom. "But first we need to wash our hands."

Lizzy pulled a chair up in front of the sink and then helped Emily to kneel on it so she could reach the faucet. Together they washed their hands.

Then, while Emily took care of the rolls, Lizzy dipped up the corn in a serving bowl. Beside the plates on the table, everyone had a bowl for the chicken and dumplings. She would fill them from the large pot on the stove once the other two were seated.

"Look, Daddy, I'm helping," Emily said as Clint returned to the kitchen with the booster seat in hand.

"That's great, bug," he replied as he buckled the seat onto a chair.

"I'm done, Ms. Lizzy," Emily said when all the rolls were in the basket.

"Thank you for your help," Lizzy replied. "You did a great job." She removed the baking sheet from the table and then gestured for Clint to sit.

Within minutes they were all seated at the table with the food served. "Oh my gosh, this is absolutely delicious," he said. He offered her a wide smile. "It definitely beats chicken from a box."

Lizzy laughed. "I'm glad you like it."

"I definitely like it," he replied. There was a warmth in his eyes when he gazed at her, a warmth that shot a shiver of sweet delight through her.

"I like it," Emily said with a rivulet of chicken broth running down her chin.

"Use your napkin, bug," Clint said to his daughter. She grabbed her napkin and did a quick swipe at her mouth.

"Bug... Is that Emily's official nickname?" Lizzy asked.

"I'm bug," Emily said proudly. "I'm Daddy's bug."

"I started calling her my bug when she was about two years old and into virtually everything. I figured *bug* was better than *cockroach*."

Lizzy laughed again. "*Bug* is definitely better."

"What about you? Did your parents have a nickname for you when you were young?"

"My mother passed away when I was eleven, of kidney disease," she replied. "But Lizzy is a nickname. My real name is Elizabeth."

"I'm so sorry to hear about your mother," he said.

"Thanks, but it was a long time ago."

"So you were basically raised by only your father and you seem to have turned out all right." He shot a quick glance at his daughter. She saw the deep concern that darkened his eyes.

"You seem to be doing a great job. All that's important is that she knows you love her, and that's obvious," Lizzy said.

He nodded. "I just worry sometimes that as she gets older, I won't be enough."

Once again, Lizzy wondered about his ex-wife. She'd love to ask him more questions about her, but certainly couldn't do that with Emily present. However, the little girl didn't seem to be paying any attention to their conversation as she chased dumplings around in her bowl with her spoon.

"I'm sure it will be just fine," she said. "And maybe sometime in the future you'll find a nice woman and she'll be a partner and helpmate for you as Emily gets older."

"I don't really see another marriage in my future," he replied.

That was definitely not what Lizzy wanted to hear and it made her even more curious about his marriage to Emily's mother and why he had no desire to take another wife. He was a relatively young man. She assumed he was in his mid-thirties and he would probably make somebody a good husband.

"Can I have another roll?" Emily asked.

"Absolutely," Lizzy replied and passed the basket to her. "Would you like some more chicken, too?" Emily's bowl was now empty.

"Maybe a little bit," she said.

"More, please," Clint said with a twinkle in his eyes as he held his dish out, too.

Lizzy laughed and got up to refill their bowls. It was the best testimony that they were enjoying the meal. The conversation was once again light and easy as they finished up the meal.

"Just leave everything," she said once they were done eating. "I can do the cleanup later. How about a cup of coffee and dessert in the living room? We've got crumb cake and fresh apple pie."

"Can I have both?" Emily asked.

"Did you make the pie?" Clint asked.

"I did," she replied.

"Then, I'll just take the apple pie," he replied.

"I'll get everything together and bring it into the living room," she said.

"That sounds great, but I am not leaving everything for you to clean up." He rose from the table. "If I help, it will only take a couple of minutes."

"It's really not necessary," Lizzy protested. "I can clear it after you and Emily go home."

"You cooked, it's only right that I help with the cleanup." As if to prove his point, he picked up his bowl and plate and carried them to the sink.

"Well, if you insist," she finally capitulated. "Emily, I bought you a coloring book and crayons. They're on the coffee table in the living room," Lizzy said. She'd specifically made a quick trip into town the day before to get the items for the little girl.

"I love to color," Emily said as Clint helped her

down from the booster seat. She immediately bee-lined out of the kitchen.

"I really appreciate how kind you're being to Emily," he said as he continued to clear the table with her.

"She's really easy to be nice to. She's a real sweet-heart and you've done a great job with her."

"Thanks. She's definitely the most important per-son in my life," he replied.

"As she should be," Lizzy responded. Each time he got close to her, her head dizzied with the scent of him. "I might be getting too personal, and if I am, please tell me to mind my own business. I was won-dering what happened to Emily's mother? Does she ever see Emily?"

She immediately felt an edge of tension emanate from him. "No, she's completely out of Emily's life. Unfortunately, my ex-wife enjoyed drugs more than her family. I tried to get her help again and again, but in the end, I realized I couldn't help her. By the time we divorced, she was heavy into meth, so I pe-titioned the court for full custody of Emily and won."

"I'm sorry. That's so sad. Do you ever hear from her?"

"No, she's never contacted me or Emily since the day our divorce was final. Truthfully, I don't even know whether she's dead or alive." He released a deep sigh. "I've told Emily her mother is up in heaven and she loves Emily very much."

"Do you ever plan to tell her the truth?" Lizzy

stacked all the china plates and bowls in one side of the sink. She never put them in the dishwasher. She would hand wash them when her company was gone.

Clint carried the cranberry salad to the counter and then leaned with one hip against the cabinet. "I grapple with that question every night. To be honest, I don't know if I will ever tell her the truth. If I do, it will definitely be when she is much older so she can truly understand."

He went back to the table and grabbed the butter dish. "Thank you for sharing that with me," she said.

"No problem. It was a painful part of my past, but it's over now. What about you? Do you have any deep, dark secrets to hide?"

She laughed. "Nope. With me it's what you see is what you get."

His gaze held hers for a long moment. "I like that about you," he said.

"Thanks," she replied with a half-breathless laugh. Oh, the man was definitely drawing her in. So far, she hadn't found a single thing that might turn her off and away from him. "Why don't you go on into the living room and I'll bring the coffee out?"

"That sounds good." He grabbed the booster seat from the chair.

He left the kitchen and it felt as if he took all the energy in the room with him. It had been a very long time since she'd liked a man as much as she liked Clint. He intrigued her and excited her and she could only hope he felt the same way about her.

Sure, it bothered her a bit that he'd said he didn't see another marriage in his future, but it was way too early for her to be thinking about a marriage with him. For goodness' sake, she barely knew the man.

She made the coffee and then carried the two cups into the living room, where Emily was seated on the floor coloring and he sat on the sofa. She handed him one and then returned with the dessert. Once they had everything, she joined him on the sofa with her coffee.

"I forgot to tell you. Emily and I had an interview this morning with Rosa Mendoza," he said as he cut into the apple pie and took a bite.

"How did it go?" she asked.

"Great, I have her starting work for me tomorrow. Thank you for referring her to me. I think she's going to be a great fit for us. And this pie is absolutely delicious."

"Yeah, delicious," Emily echoed.

"Thanks, and now back to Rosa. She's a good woman. I'm sure you won't be sorry." She paused and took a sip of her coffee. "Have you thought about who you might want to help you with harvesting your corn or are you doing it yourself?"

"No, I'm certainly not doing it myself. As far as I know, I don't own a combine. As for who I might hire, the problem is I don't really know anyone around here except for you."

"For the last couple of years, I've had Jerry West harvest mine. He's an old-timer who helps several people out. He's reasonable and reliable and he has a small team of men who get the job done quickly. If you want me to, I'll text you his number later today."

"Thanks, I don't know what I'd do without you, Lizzy. I definitely need to get out and meet more people."

She smiled. "You might want to hang out at the feed store or spend an evening at the Farmer's Club."

"The Farmer's Club? What is that?" he asked curiously.

"We have two bars here in Millsville. Murphy's is big and noisy and most of the young, single people hang out there. On the other hand, the Farmer's Club is a smaller, more intimate bar. The older crowd tend to go there."

"Which one do you prefer?"

She laughed. "A couple of years ago my best friend and I spent a lot of time at Murphy's, but I don't go there much anymore. These days I much prefer the Farmer's Club for a quiet drink and a little downtime."

"Maybe some evening I could have Rosa stay late and you and I could go to the Farmer's Club together."

A sweet warmth swept through her. "I'd like that."

"Look, Ms. Lizzy, I finished my picture," Emily said.

"Honey, that's really pretty. You did a good job staying in the lines," Lizzy replied.

Emily sat back on her haunches and looked around

the room. "Look, Daddy. Look at all the little cows." She pointed to the cow collection on the bookshelves.

"My daddy collected them," Lizzy explained.

"Where is your daddy?" Emily asked.

"He's up in heaven," Lizzy replied.

"My mommy is in heaven, too. Maybe they're friends there," Emily said with a smile.

Lizzy returned her smile. "That would be lovely."

"This has been nice," Clint said and rose from the sofa. "But, it's time for us to go. Let's just get these dishes back into the kitchen."

"I insist you not do that," Lizzy replied. "I can take care of this."

"I wanna stay here with Ms. Lizzy," Emily said.

"Emily, I promise you we'll plan a day to spend together. My friend owns the nail shop in town. Maybe we could plan to go into her place and have our fingernails and toes done."

"Yes." Emily clapped her hands together in obvious excitement. "Can she do pink like my daddy does?"

"Absolutely she does pink. We can get our nails painted the same pretty color," Lizzy replied.

"Oh goody," Emily exclaimed and clapped her hands together once again. "And then we'll match."

"Now, put the crayons back in the box and then it's time for us to go home," Clint said.

As Emily got busy picking up, Clint smiled at Lizzy. God, she loved his smile. It never failed to shoot a rivulet of warmth through her.

"Thank you for the delicious meal and dessert and the wonderful company," he said.

"It has been my pleasure," she replied.

By that time Emily had finished and the three of them walked out the front door and into the afternoon sunshine. Clint carried the booster seat out and Emily walked next to him.

"I'll text you Jerry's number later," Lizzy said.

He nodded. "Thanks again for everything. Emily, what do you say to Ms. Lizzy?"

"I love your chicken, Ms. Lizzy," she said. Clint and Lizzy laughed.

"That's good enough for me," Lizzy said.

They said their goodbyes and she remained on the porch as they got into the truck and then drove down the driveway. She stayed outside, even after they arrived at their house.

She raised her face to the sun as a wave of happiness flooded through her veins. She wasn't sure she'd ever felt this way so quickly about a man. Clint made her feel giddy and girly and he filled her with a sweet anticipation as to what might happen next between them.

Would he actually invite her to the Farmer's Club? Did he want to see her again as much as she wanted to see him? One thing was for sure, she would definitely plan a day with Emily. She'd make sure the two of them went to Sassy Nails and got pedis and manis.

A cold chill suddenly washed over her as the hair on the nape of her neck rose up. She looked around but saw nothing amiss. Still, she had the distinct feeling of somebody watching her.

She was in the middle of nowhere, but there were plenty of trees and bushes for somebody to hide behind. Her heart began to beat erratically, and the back of her throat closed up with alarm.

She quickly whirled around and went back into her house. She locked the door and then leaned against it as she waited for her heartbeat to slow to a more normal rhythm.

Was Butch hiding out there somewhere, intent on bullying her about the town budget? She suspected it had been Butch who had made the nasty phone calls to her. Was he stepping up his game now? Trying to freak her out to punish her for not voting in the budget?

Or was it possible the Scarecrow Killer was out there, watching her every move and just waiting for the perfect opportunity to grab her and turn her into one of his horrid scarecrow collection?

Chapter 5

Rosa Mendoza was a dream come true. While Clint was out working in the fields, she got Emily off to school in the mornings and then she returned in the afternoons and picked her up from the bus stop after school. She also prepared their evening meal for them. After the first few days, Emily adored the older woman but was still absolutely crazy about Ms. Lizzy.

Ms. Lizzy had been on his mind, too. He'd enjoyed the dinner at her house. The chicken and dumplings had been delicious and the cranberry salad had been quite tasty, but what he enjoyed more than the food was just being with her.

There was an easiness with her. The conversation

flowed between them without any difficulty and they laughed together often.

As a matter of fact, he couldn't wait to see her again. With that thought in mind, that Thursday as Rosa served the evening meal, he decided to ask her if she could stay late on Friday night.

"It wouldn't be a real late night…maybe eleven or so," he said to the plump, gray-haired woman. "And that's just if Lizzy is available to go out."

"I wanna go out with Ms. Lizzy," Emily said.

"Not this time, bug. We're going to a place where only grown-ups are allowed," he replied and then looked back at Rosa.

"Hmm, do I smell a bit of romance in the air?" Rosa asked, her dark eyes twinkling.

"Uh, no, just a growing friendship," he replied. He couldn't get into a romance. It would be too dangerous. It was bad enough that he'd invited Rosa into their lives, but he'd needed her.

However, he'd sensed when he met her that she was not a snooper, and the deal was she'd cook the evening meal but not be responsible for any housekeeping except for the kitchen area.

Therefore, there was no reason for her to ever go back into his bedroom. There was a file folder in there that he never wanted anyone to see. It was bad enough that he felt the need to look at it as often as he did.

"I can stay late," Rosa replied. "You know Lizzy is a wonderful woman," she continued. "She's well-liked by everyone who knows her around town. And on that note, I'll just be on my way."

Clint didn't know if her words were an endorsement of Lizzy or a warning to him not to mess around or play games with her.

The agreement they had set up when he'd hired Rosa was that she cooked and served the evening meal and then he was responsible for the final cleanup, although she often scrubbed whatever pots and pans there were before he got to them.

"Good night, Rosa," he said. "As usual, thanks for everything."

"Bye, Ms. Rosa," Emily said around a mouthful of mashed potatoes.

"I'll see you both in the morning," Rosa replied and then she was gone.

"I like Ms. Rosa, Daddy, but I love Ms. Lizzy," Emily said.

"That's nice to know," Clint replied.

"I think Ms. Lizzy would make a really good mommy," Emily said and released a big sigh.

"Honey, I told you before. Ms. Lizzy is just a friend and neighbor, but she isn't going to be your mommy."

"I know." She sighed again and then stabbed her fork into the meatloaf. "But I can always wish for it," she added slightly under her breath.

It was after he tucked Emily in bed later that evening that he sank down on the sofa and grabbed his phone. It was short notice to ask Lizzy out for the next night. Hopefully she hadn't already made plans with somebody else. He was surprised to realize the thought of her going out with another man disturbed him more than he wanted to admit.

He punched in her number and she answered on the second ring. "Hi, neighbor," she said.

Her voice caused a rush of warmth to fill the pit of his stomach. "Hi back at you," he said. "I wanted to thank you for sending Jerry West my way. I'm now on his schedule when harvest time rolls around."

"That's great," she replied. "He's a good man and a really hard worker."

"Uh, I was wondering if you're free tomorrow night and you could show me the Farmer's Club. Maybe we could chill there and have a drink or two."

"I'm definitely free and I would love to go with you," she replied.

"Great, why don't I pick you up around seven?"

"Perfect, I'll be ready."

They said their goodbyes and the call ended. He knew he shouldn't be seeing Lizzy in a social way, especially since he couldn't wait to be with her again.

Maybe he could date her without giving her anything real about his past. Surely he was intelligent enough to keep his cover in place with her. It wasn't like they were going to get married. They were just having a pleasant time hanging out together.

The next evening at precisely seven, he pulled up in front of Lizzy's house. She stepped out the front door and his breath caught in his throat at how beautiful she looked.

She was clad in a tight pair of jeans that showcased her long, slender legs. She also had on a long-sleeved royal blue blouse that he knew would perfectly match her gorgeous blue eyes. Her hair was loose around her shoulders and looked shiny and silky in the waning sunshine.

He started to get out, but before he could, she ran to the passenger side, opened the door and slid in. "Hi," she said with her bright smile that always warmed him.

"Hi, yourself," he replied. He waited for her to buckle her seat belt and then he pulled out of her driveway and headed toward town.

"How was your week?" he asked.

"Productive," she replied. "I set up three interviews for next week in hopes of hiring a couple of new ranch hands. I've also begun the task of cleaning up my barn in anticipation of ordering hay for the winter."

"Wow, you have been busy. I definitely need to get into my barn. It was left a mess when I bought the place and I'm not even sure what's out there right now."

"The former owners were an older couple who had pretty much given up on things months before you took over the place," she replied.

"Yeah, there was a lot of cleanup to do just in the house alone. I'd still like to buy some new furniture for the living room. I think the sofa and chair that are in there now are probably from the fifties."

She laughed. "I get it. I bought a lot of new things after my father passed away. Like you, I think the furniture that was in there before I replaced it was at least twenty-five years old."

"Change is sometimes hard," he said. "I'm still finding my way as a new farmer and rancher."

"You made a really big one, coming from corporate California to live here in the middle of nowhere."

"I like it here in the middle of nowhere." He tightened his hands on the steering wheel as he thought of the reason he was in a small town in Kansas. He had to keep reminding himself that he and Emily were safe in Millsville. He wouldn't have invited Lizzy into his life in any way if he thought they weren't safe here or if he thought she might be in danger.

"I'm so glad you like it here," she replied.

He definitely liked her. Her scent filled the cab of the truck, that evocative scent that drew him in. Her nearness to him warmed and excited him. Oh yes…he definitely liked her a lot.

"You're going to have to give me some directions to the Farmer's Club. I don't remember seeing it on Main Street," he said.

"It's a block off Main. I'll tell you where to turn when we get a little closer," she said. "I was wondering if maybe tomorrow afternoon I could pick up Emily and take her to the nail shop?"

"That would be really nice. I know she would

absolutely love it. You do realize she's crazy about you."

"I think she's a very sweet, well-behaved little girl and I'm pretty crazy about her, too. Why don't I pick her up around one thirty? My best friend, Bailey Troy, owns the nail salon and she'll see to it that Emily really gets the royal treatment."

"That's really considerate of you," he replied. Her kindness to his daughter made him like her even more. He didn't think she was faking her feelings for Emily, either. They felt very genuine and real.

They reached town and he hadn't driven very far up Main Street when she told him to turn left at the next intersection. She had to point out the Farmer's Club as it was really nothing more than a little hole in the wall.

He parked along the curb and after they got out, it felt only natural for him to take her hand in his as they walked up the sidewalk. He liked the way her fingers entwined with his and the utter softness of her skin.

The exterior of the Farmer's Club was definitely restrained. The dark blinds at the window were closed and only a small neon beer sign indicated that it was a bar.

Reluctantly he dropped her hand to open the door and usher her inside. Once in, he looked around the place with interest. There was a long, polished bar against one side of the room and booths and tables on the other side. In the back he could see an area for shuffleboard and an electronic dartboard hung on the wall. The air smelled of bar food and beer.

An old country song played softly overhead and the noise level in the bar was low and conducive to conversation. She led him to a booth midway between the front door and the activities in the back.

"Is this okay?" she asked.

"Looks perfect to me," he replied. He waited until she slid into one side and then he slid into the other.

The bartender immediately came to the side of the table. "Hey, Lizzy," he greeted.

"Hi, Ranger. This is Clint Kincaid, the new guy in town. Clint, this is Ranger Simmons, the owner of this place," she said.

The two men shook hands. "Nice to meet you, Clint. What are you doing hanging out with this rabble-rouser?"

Lizzy laughed. "I beg your pardon?" She raised her chin with mock indignation.

"I heard about your dealings with the city council members. Butch was in the other night and was cursing you up one side and down the other." Ranger smiled at her warmly. "That's how I knew you were doing something right. Keep fighting for all of us little folk who can't afford higher taxes."

"That's my plan," Lizzy replied.

"Good, now what can I get for you two to drink?" Ranger asked.

"I'd like a beer," Lizzy said, and named the brand that she liked.

"Make that two," Clint said.

"Got it. I'll be right back with your beers," Ranger said.

"I didn't have you pegged as a beer drinker," Clint said once Ranger left their booth.

"Normally I'm a margarita kind of girl, but tonight a beer just sounded good," she replied. "I like a beer on a warm summer day, but when winter comes along, I'm more of a mixed-drink kind of gal."

"I agree with you about a beer on a summer day. But I also like a beer on a cold, wintry night," he replied. "It won't be long before winter will be here."

"Please, don't remind me," she replied. "I don't like winters, but I do like curling up under a warm blanket with a roaring fire in the fireplace."

"I definitely agree with you on that," he replied.

A few minutes later they had their drinks in front of them. "I can see why this is a nice place to come and have a drink and unwind after a workday," he said.

"I like it here. It's not too noisy and sometimes the old-timers come in. I enjoy talking to them and picking their brains about crops and cows. This is a place where I don't feel odd about being alone."

He grinned. "And now you're here with somebody who can't offer you anything in the way of tips or wisdom about crops and cows."

She laughed. "Sometimes a girl just needs a night off."

"So, tell me more about this city council thing, and who is Butch?" he said.

"Butch is a blowhard who likes to get his own way."

As she explained it all to him, he loved watching the expressions that crossed her features. Her face was so animated, and he had a feeling you always knew what she was feeling at any moment.

"I'm proud of you for standing up for the people of Millsville," he said when she was finished explaining everything.

"I just know what's right," she replied. "And what they're presenting as a budget just isn't right at this point in time. Now, let's talk about something more pleasant. How is Emily doing in school?"

"Great. She's made some new friends and she is getting lots of happy faces from the teacher. And speaking of Emily, her birthday is next Friday. You don't happen to know anyone who has puppies for sale, do you? I've been looking in the paper, and so far, I haven't seen anything."

"Actually, I do know somebody. Gladys Singer is a dog breeder and she's my neighbor on the other side. She mentioned to me the other day that she'll have a litter of Chihuahuas ready to be sold this week. Are you planning any kind of a birthday party for her?"

"Not really. I ordered a cake from the Sweet Tooth Bakery and I planned to take her to the gazebo in the center of town to eat it. I'd love for you to join us and Emily would be so happy if you could be there. But if we could go to your neighbor's, and she gets to pick out a puppy at the end of it all, it would absolutely make her day."

"I'm pretty sure I can arrange it with Gladys and I'd love to eat cake with you and Emily in the gazebo," she replied.

"I swear, Lizzy, I don't know what I'd do without you," he said. "All I have to do is ask and you give it to me. I've been really worried about the puppy thing. You're like a genie in the bottle who makes wishes come true."

She grinned. "A bottle would be way too small to hold me. The truth of the matter is I just know a lot of people."

"That has certainly worked to my advantage." He paused and took a drink of his beer, then put the bottle back down. "So, what's new in Lizzy Maxwell's world?"

"Not much. Like I told you earlier, I've got some interviews set up for next week and I'm looking forward to getting some help around the ranch. Maybe you should consider doing the same thing. Your spread is awfully big for one person to take care of."

"I keep telling myself I just need to hang on through the winter months and then I'll hire some help next spring," he replied.

"That sounds like a plan, but you do realize there's a lot of work to be done even in the winter months."

"Duly noted," he replied. "So, tell me more about you."

She grinned. "I'm a Libra who likes food and riding my horse, Sunshine, across the pasture. And what sign are you?" She fluttered her eyelashes and gave him a vacuous gaze.

He laughed. "I'm a Leo who likes food and I'm learning to enjoy riding my horse, Diamond. I was actually thinking of something a little deeper than that," he replied. "Tell me about your father."

She took a long drink of her beer and then told him about how her father had changed after her mother's passing and then how she had nursed him for two years until his death.

It was definitely a window into her soul and showed him what he'd already suspected, that she was a loving, caring person. But he also saw a hint of pain in her eyes as she spoke of him. "It was like when my mother died, my father died with her," she said.

He got it. Her father had let her down. When she'd needed him most after the death of her mother, he'd been absent and had remained absent until his own death. His heart hurt for the little girl who had basically raised herself without the love and support of a parent.

"What about your folks?" she asked when she was finished sharing about hers.

"They passed away in a drunk-driver wreck five years ago. They were coming home after having dinner at their favorite restaurant. They were at a stop sign when the other driver slammed into the back of them. The police believed the driver had to have been traveling at a speed well over a hundred miles an hour. Mom and Dad were immediately pronounced dead at the scene."

Unexpected emotion crawled up the back of his throat. He tried not to think about that time. He'd thought nothing else he would ever experience could be worse than that, but he'd been so wrong. Still, he was almost grateful that his parents hadn't been alive when Samantha had been murdered. They had loved his wife and would have been devastated by what had happened to her.

Lizzy must have seen his pain, for she reached out and took his hand in hers. "So, we're both orphans now," she said softly. "And I'm so sorry about your parents. Drunk drivers are the absolute worst." She held his hand for only a moment and then she pulled hers away.

For the next hour they talked about more pleasant things. He confessed how hard it had been for him to get up on the back of a horse the first time, and he had her laughing and so he embellished the story to make her laugh even harder.

She introduced him to more people as they stopped by the booth to say hello to her. By that time, ten-thirty had rolled around and they decided to call it a night.

"This has been so lovely," she said once they were in the truck and headed back home.

"It has been really nice," he agreed. He felt as if they now knew each other on a deeper level, and it felt good. He'd encouraged her to talk about her life in hopes that she wouldn't ask too many about his past. For the most part, it had worked.

"I agree with you that the Farmer's Club is a great place to relax and have a drink."

"I enjoy it occasionally," she replied.

"On another note, I heard there's a cool front moving in this week. It will be a welcome relief after all this heat," he said.

"Autumn is my favorite time of year," she replied. "I love the changing colors of the leaves and the cooler nights. I even like the way autumn smells."

"Since I've never enjoyed a real fall, I'm looking forward to it." There was a part of him that hated how easy it was becoming to lie. He had enjoyed lots of beautiful autumns in New York. It had been Samantha's favorite time of the year, too.

"Winters out here can be pretty rough," she said. "The California man needs to be prepared for freezing temperatures and lots and lots of snow."

"This California man is definitely trying to prepare himself for that."

"In the wintertime, it's all about the cattle and horses. They need water that isn't frozen and plenty of hay put out for them to eat. And that's just to start with," she said.

"You've talked me into seeing about finding some help before winter sets in," he replied.

As they got closer to her house, a nervous tension rose up inside him. With her scent surrounding him and the new closeness he felt toward her, his desire in this moment was to get a kiss good-night from her.

He shot a surreptitious glance at her. In the soft lighting from the dashboard, she looked beautiful and his desire for her only rose higher inside him.

God, it had been a long time since he'd felt this way about a woman. Lizzy tapped into feelings and emotions he'd forgotten that he could possess.

Suddenly they were at her house and as he thought about the possibility of a kiss, his palms became clammy and his heart raced.

They got out of the truck and he walked her to her front porch. "Do you still want me to join you for Emily's birthday party?" she asked.

"Absolutely," he replied.

"I'll text you Gladys's phone number tomorrow so you can talk to her about her puppies."

"That would be great. Why don't I pick you up around five-thirty on Friday and we'll go from there."

"Perfect," she replied. "I'll be ready for the birthday girl."

She definitely looked perfect under the glow of her porch light. "I really enjoyed this evening with you," he said and took a step closer to her.

"So did I."

"Lizzy, uh, can I kiss you good-night?"

"I would like that," she replied without hesitation.

He meant for it to be a simple touching of the lips, but as she leaned into him, he wrapped his arms around her and drew her closer…closer still.

She opened her mouth as if in open invitation and he accepted, deepening the kiss by swirling his tongue with hers. She tasted of hot desire and her body fit perfectly against his.

She definitely knew how to kiss and he wanted to hold her and kiss her forever, but when he realized he was getting quite aroused and he felt things starting to spiral out of control, he reluctantly dropped his arms to his sides and the kiss ended.

"Oh, Lizzy, I could definitely get used to kissing you," he said.

"The feeling is mutual," she replied, her voice half-breathless.

"Good to know." His blood heated inside his veins. "Then, I'll see you tomorrow when you pick up Emily for your spa day."

"I look forward to it." She turned and unlocked her door and then with a murmured goodbye, she disappeared into her house.

He walked back to his truck with the imprint of her mouth still lingering on his. Was it possible he could have a real relationship with Lizzy and still keep his disguise in place? He was beginning to believe so.

Really, only time would tell, but one thing was for certain… He couldn't wait to see her…to kiss her again.

The kiss sealed it. He nearly jumped out of the bush with glee as he watched the two of them kiss.

There was desire in their kiss. It was obvious to any onlooker that they were deeply into each other.

Clint Kincaid's fate had been sealed since that night almost four years ago. The fact that he cared about Lizzy Maxwell was simply icing on the cake.

It was time to start to make the proper preparations. It was time he got all his ducks in a row so he could exact the revenge he so desired, the retribution he'd dreamed about for the last almost-four years.

He couldn't wait. It was going to be bloody and heinous and he absolutely couldn't wait.

Chapter 6

The next afternoon as Lizzy left her house to drive over to Clint's to pick up Emily for their spa day together, her thoughts were definitely on Emily's father.

Their kiss the night before had curled her toes with pleasure and rocked her world. She couldn't wait for another opportunity for him to kiss her again. She loved to kiss and she couldn't imagine being with somebody who didn't do it well. Clint definitely did it very well.

He was so easy to talk to and funny, too. Their senses of humor were alike, and she found that sexy as hell. He'd been very sweet when she'd been talking about her father and her life after her mother's death.

For the first time in a long time, she was excited

about a man and she was hoping her relationship with Clint would only grow and deepen. She felt like he could possibly be the one, her person who would understand her and enrich her life. The idea of him being her person filled her with excitement. She'd been looking for her person for a very long time.

She pulled up in front of his house and before she could get out of the car, Emily ran out of the front door. Clint followed just behind her.

"Ms. Lizzy, Ms. Lizzy, I'm ready to go," Emily said excitedly. "I'm all ready. I got my favorite blue clothes on today, and everything."

"I see that," Lizzy said with a laugh. The little girl looked cute as a button in a blue dress that matched her pretty eyes, and her long blond hair was pulled up into a ponytail.

"Hi, Lizzy," Clint said. His gaze was warm as it lingered on her.

"Good afternoon," she replied with a smile.

"Before you leave, I need to get the car seat out of my truck and put it in yours," he said.

"That would be wise. I don't want Dallas to ticket me because I don't have the proper equipment to carry precious cargo."

"Dallas?" He looked at her curiously.

"Dallas Calloway. He's the chief of police," she explained as she walked with him over to his truck. Emily danced after them, obviously eager to get the show on the road.

"I haven't met him yet." He opened the back door and leaned in to unfasten the car seat.

"He's a really nice guy, but he's got his hands full right now with the scarecrow thing," she replied.

"I hope you're keeping yourself safe."

"I'll tell you a little secret. I've taken to carrying a little revolver in my purse," she said. "Does that bother you?"

She'd made the decision to carry her gun because there had been several times when she'd been out and about the ranch where she got the distinct feeling that she was being watched. She really didn't believe it was Butch, and she wasn't sure if it was just a figment of her imagination or not, but she wasn't willing to take any chances.

"Does it bother me?" He straightened with the car seat in his arms. "It would only bother me if, at some point in time, you decide to use it on me."

She laughed. "I think you're safe." She sobered. "I would only use it if I feared for my very life."

"Actually, I'm glad you're taking your safety seriously," he replied. "I think it is especially important since you're a particular type." She knew he was talking about the fact that she was blond-haired and blue-eyed, exactly the killer's preference.

They walked back to her truck, where he fastened in the car seat. He'd barely gotten it done when Emily climbed up and buckled herself in. "I'm ready," she proclaimed.

"I hope you girls have a wonderful time," he said.

"I'm going to get started with the cleanup in my barn while you two are gone. That's probably going to take days to complete. And once that's done, then I'll know…"

"Daddy… Daddy, stop, please stop talking," Emily said in obvious aggravation. "We need to go now."

Lizzy and Clint both laughed. "I guess we'd better get this party started," she replied and opened the driver's door. She slid in behind the steering wheel and then started the car and rolled down her window.

"We'll be gone for a couple of hours," she said. He waved and nodded and then she pulled away.

Immediately she was inundated with all things Emily. The little girl talked about her school and all her new friends. She told Lizzy that she loved ladybugs and butterflies and how much she wanted a puppy for her birthday.

"You know a puppy is a big responsibility," Lizzy chimed in. "You have to feed them and clean up after them. When your puppy poops, who is going to pick that up?"

"Daddy?"

"Whose puppy will it be?" Lizzy countered.

"Mine."

"Then, who should pick up the poop?"

"So, I pick up the poop," Emily replied with a giggle. "I'll pick up the puppy's poop and I'll love the puppy."

"That's the most important thing of all. What else do you want for your birthday?"

The drive into town went quickly with Emily chattering happily all the way.

Lizzy was enchanted with Emily, who was bright and funny and loving. Of course, she reminded herself that she hadn't seen what happened when Emily didn't get her way or when she was angry. Maybe behind closed doors she threw terrible temper tantrums.

Today it was all smiles and happy conversation. By the time she pulled up and parked just down the street from the Sassy Nail Salon, Lizzy was almost as excited as Emily was about the day.

She got Emily out of the vehicle and then grabbed her hand as they walked the short distance toward the front door. Almost immediately Lizzy got a chill and the hairs on the nape of her neck stood up.

It was that familiar sense of being watched. She turned around and looked behind them but saw nothing and nobody out of the ordinary. It was the same odd feeling she'd gotten before.

The same questions flew through her head. Was she somehow being stalked by somebody or was it all just her imagination working overtime? Was her fear of becoming the Scarecrow Killer's next victim making her overly paranoid? She wasn't sure what to believe.

She definitely breathed a sigh of relief as they walked through the front door of the shop and Bailey greeted them. "So, this is the little princess who is getting her nails done for the very first time," Bailey said. She leaned down. "Hi, Emily, my name is Bailey and I'm a good friend of Lizzy's."

"I love Ms. Lizzy," Emily replied with an adoring look at Lizzy.

"That makes two of us because I love her, too," Bailey said. "Now, let's take you to your chair so we can get your feet soaking."

"My feet?" Emily looked at her in surprise.

"We always soak our feet when we're getting a pedicure," Lizzy explained.

"Are you going to do that?" Emily asked Lizzy with a touch of worry in her voice.

"Absolutely, and I'll be sitting right next to you," Lizzy replied.

"That's good," Emily replied.

Bailey had gone all out. The chair she led Emily to had a pink, fuzzy boa decorating it, and once she got Emily's shoes and socks off and her feet were in the water, she placed a little tiara on her head.

"Look, Ms. Lizzy, I'm a princess," Emily exclaimed with a huge smile.

"Yes, you are," Lizzy agreed as she lowered her bare feet into the water bowl next to the little girl's chair.

The afternoon was delightful. Emily giggled as her feet were scrubbed and then her little toenails were painted a pretty pink. "You tickled me," she said to Bailey, who was taking care of Emily.

Bailey laughed. "I always tickle little feet. It's part of my job."

While they were getting the works, Lizzy and Bailey spoke in code since they were within earshot of Emily. "Is he still Mr. Perfect?" Bailey asked.

"Absolutely," Lizzy replied. "So far, not a wiggling ear in sight."

Bailey laughed. "Aside from the budding romance, what else is new in your life?"

"I've got those three interviews lined up on Wednesday. Are you still coming over to sit with me?"

"Absolutely. What time is the first interview?"

"I've got them set up for nine, ten and eleven," Lizzy said.

"I'm assuming you're offering me an amazing lunch that day after the interviews are all done," Bailey replied.

"Probably sandwiches of some sort."

"I like samwiches," Emily said. "I like peanut-butter-and-jelly samwiches."

"Me, too," Bailey said as she began to paint Emily's fingernails.

One of the other girls worked on Lizzy's nails. She was also getting a pretty pink to match Emily's. The afternoon flew by with lots of giggles and conversations fit for a five-year-old. The other nail artists who worked for Bailey joined in the fun, keeping Emily happy and smiling throughout the afternoon.

When the nail experience was finished, Emily danced out of the shop with her tiara still on her head. "That was so fun," she said, and to Lizzy's surprise, the little girl wrapped her arms around Lizzy's waist and hugged her tight.

"I love you so much, Ms. Lizzy. I wish you could be my mommy. Even though I have one up in heaven, I need a mommy here with me."

The hug and the words Emily spoke pulled a lump into the back of Lizzy's throat. "Oh, honey, maybe someday your daddy will get you a new mommy," Lizzy said as she gently unwound Emily's arms from around her.

"How can he do that?" Emily asked as they continued on to the truck.

"Well, he would have to fall in love with a woman and then marry her," Lizzy replied. "And then she would be your mommy."

They reached the truck and she opened the back door and helped Emily get into her car seat. Lizzy was grateful that she didn't have that crazy feeling of somebody watching her now. Everything felt wonderfully normal.

On the drive home Emily talked about the nail experience.

She liked Bailey and she giggled as she talked about her pedicure. "My toes got tickled so much," she said, making Lizzy laugh with her.

"Now when I go to school I can show my new pretty pink nails to Justin," Emily said.

"Who is Justin?"

"He's a boy who is sometimes mean to me, but I like him."

"What is Justin's last name?" Lizzy asked.

"Last name? I don't know about his last name. But my name used to be Natalie before," the little girl said.

"What do you mean?" Lizzy asked in confusion.

"I was Natalie before and now I'm Emily. I liked Natalie way better, but Daddy said it was time for me to be Emily."

"I think Emily is a really pretty name," Lizzy replied, but the whole conversation was confusing. Why would she have to change her name? It was an odd thing for the little girl to say.

She continued to turn it over in her head as she drove back to Clint's place. Once there, she parked and got out of the truck. Clint walked out of the nearby barn to greet them.

He looked totally hot in a pair of overalls that displayed his wide shoulders and fit arms. A couple strands of hay clung to the top of his black hair. He looked like a model who had just leaped from the pages of a sexy-farmer calendar.

"Hey, princess, did you have a good time?" he asked Emily as she got out of the car seat and exited the truck.

"I had fun, fun, fun!" she exclaimed. "Daddy, you need to marry Ms. Lizzy so she'll be my mommy forever."

A blush filled Lizzy cheeks with fiery heat as Clint stared at her and an uncomfortable silence ensued.

* * *

What had Lizzy been telling his daughter? He stared at Lizzy in confusion. "Daddy, look at my pretty pink fingernails, and my toenails match them," Emily said, breaking the silence that had built up. Emily held her fingernails out for him to see.

"They look absolutely beautiful," he said.

"They tickled my feet and then painted my toenails pretty pink, too."

"And I see you have a crown to officially make you a princess for the day," he said.

"I'll just take off now," Lizzy said.

"No, wait, please. Come in and have a cup of coffee or a cold drink," he said to her.

"I've got to show my baby dolls my new nails," Emily said and took off running for the front door.

"I just want you to know I didn't prompt Emily in any way to say anything about you marrying me," Lizzy said, a blush coloring her cheeks again. "She asked me how she could get a new mommy and I just told her you would have to marry a woman for that to happen."

Knowing his daughter and her love for Lizzy, he now understood exactly what had happened. "No problem," he said. "I've been inventorying the stuff in the barn for the last couple of hours. I could really use a break, so please come in for something to drink and a little conversation."

"Okay," she replied.

He ushered her into the house and to his kitchen,

where she sat at the table and he washed up in the sink. "Now…coffee or soda?" he asked.

"A soda sounds good." She looked around with interest. His kitchen was much like hers, but where hers was painted a cheerful yellow, his walls were covered in an old wallpaper with wire baskets of eggs as the pattern.

He grabbed two sodas from the fridge and joined her at the table. "Did she behave for you?"

"She was wonderfully behaved," Lizzy replied. "Everyone in the shop thought she was a little doll. Is she ever naughty?" She leaned forward, reached out and plucked a couple pieces of hay from his hair.

"Oh…thanks." The intimacy of her getting the hay out of his hair stirred him more than a little bit. "Uh, actually, Emily doesn't act up very often at all. From a very early age she knew I wouldn't tolerate temper tantrums. She responds well to reason and she's more than a bit of a people pleaser." He cracked open his soda can and she did the same.

She took a sip and then placed the can back on the table. "She did say something that was a little confusing to me on the drive back here."

"What's that?" He raised his can to his lips.

"She told me that her name used to be Natalie, but you made her change it to Emily."

Clint froze, his soda can halfway between his mouth and the table. "Oh, uh…" He slowly lowered his can back down as his brain scrambled frantically for a logical answer. "Uh, when she was very young, she heard the name Natalie on a television show and decided that should be her name. I humored her for a couple of days, but then I told her that her name was Emily and that was that."

"I guess kids can get some wild ideas in their minds," Lizzy replied and he relaxed. Thankfully she'd apparently bought his explanation.

"Definitely," he agreed. "Do you want to have children?" he asked.

Her face lit up. "In a perfect world, I'd love to be married and have two children." She looked at him curiously. "Did you ever want more children?"

"I would have liked to have at least one more so Emily would have siblings. Do you have brothers or sisters?" he asked.

"No, I'm an only child."

"Me, too," he replied. He'd once wished for brothers and sisters, but the way his life had played out, he was now grateful he had nobody close to him.

"Since you did something so nice for my daughter, I need to do something in return for you," he continued. "And since I don't really cook, the next best thing would be to take you to the café tomorrow night. Would you be up to spending more time with me and Emily?"

Once again, her features warmed. "I would love to."

"Then, why don't we plan for me to pick you up around five."

"Sounds good to me," she agreed. She drank down

the last of her soda and then stood. "On that note, I need to head home. I've got chores waiting for me there."

He got up as well and walked with her to the front door. As always, when he was around Lizzy, a swift desire for her burned in the pit of his belly.

They said their goodbyes and he closed the door behind her. She was definitely a danger to him. He liked her. He liked her a lot and he wanted their relationship to deepen, but at what cost to him?

There were so many secrets that he couldn't share with anyone…with her. If he drew her in more, then he'd just have to lie more or risk losing everything. However, the more time he spent with Lizzy, the more he considered taking a chance with her. He thought she might be worth the risk.

The next couple of days flew by. They all went out to dinner on Sunday night. It was another pleasant experience. The only thing he hated was that with Emily along he hadn't been able to kiss Lizzy again. And he definitely wanted to kiss her again.

On Wednesday morning his first thought was of Lizzy. He knew she was conducting interviews for ranch help that day and he hoped she managed to get some good help. He was seriously thinking about hiring a couple of men to assist him out on his place, too.

Despite all the books he'd read and the internet research he'd done in preparation of becoming a farmer, there were still a lot of things he just didn't know. Having a couple of experienced ranch hands working for him would probably be a good thing. He needed somebody to help him get ready for the coming winter and then be around during the cold months.

He'd already contacted Gladys Singer about the puppy for Emily and he was looking forward to seeing Lizzy on Friday evening for the birthday celebration for his daughter.

When Friday rolled around, he dressed in a royal blue polo that he knew looked good on him. He also wore a good pair of jeans and then sprayed on his favorite cologne.

Emily got home from school and he had a new little pink dress for her to wear. He loved to see her with her eyes shining brightly and excitement riding her features.

"You look like a real birthday girl," he said, once she was dressed and her hair had been brushed.

They ate sandwiches for a quick meal before heading out for her celebration. Thankfully it was a beautiful afternoon and promised to be an equally nice evening.

"Is it going to be a good birthday, Daddy? Am I going to get a puppy?" she asked as they got into his truck to leave.

"You'll just have to wait and see, bug," he replied. "First we're going to pick up Ms. Lizzy and then we're going to get your birthday cake."

He had already packed a small duffel bag with

paper plates, plastic forks and napkins so they could eat the cake in the town gazebo.

"Is my cake pink, Daddy?"

He laughed. "You just have to wait and see."

"Oh, I can't wait for everything," she replied and laughed. "I'm just too excited."

He laughed. "I'm happy you are. The big surprise is that we're going to eat our cake in the gazebo in the town square."

"The gazebo?"

"You'll see when we get there," he replied as he realized his daughter had yet to see the beautiful structure that had been built recently. "It's a really pretty place, fit for a princess."

He pulled up in front of Lizzy's house and an edge of anticipation filled him...the excitement of seeing her again, of spending time with her again. She was so bright and so much fun and so much more.

She flew out of her front door, a vibrant vision in a red-and-yellow floral dress with a lightweight yellow sweater over her shoulders. The only thing brighter than her dress was the beautiful smile she wore. Along with her purse, she carried with her a pink gift bag.

She got into the passenger side of the truck and placed the gift bag on the floorboard. "Hello, birthday girl," she said to Emily. "Are you having a good day?"

"Yes, it's a good day," she agreed. "I'm six today, Ms. Lizzy. I'm not five anymore. I'm six years old today."

"That's awesome," Lizzy said.

"What's awesome is how good you smell," he said to her softly so his daughter couldn't hear.

"Oh, thank you." Her cheeks once again filled with a charming blush. He absolutely loved her blushes. "It's my favorite perfume," she said.

"It's quickly becoming my favorite, too."

"I do believe you're flirting with me, Mr. Kincaid," she replied.

He laughed. He *was* flirting with her, and it felt good and natural. "I think I am," he agreed. "But it's been so long since I've done it, I'm not sure if I'm doing it right."

"Trust me, I'll tell you if you get it wrong," she replied with a laugh of her own.

As he drove to the Sweet Tooth Bakery, she told him about a crazy customer who had tried to burn the place down with the owner, Harper Brennan, inside.

"The good thing is she just married Sam Bravano, who is a carpenter along with his two brothers, and they've been working hard to get the place reopened again. Right now, Harper is just doing take-out orders, but I heard that she's almost ready to fully get the place running again. It was always a wonderful place to sit and have a cup of coffee with one of her sweets, and Harper is one of the really nice people in town."

"She was certainly pleasant when I called to order the cake," he replied. He turned into the parking lot of the Sweet Tooth Bakery, housed in a large yellow building with bright pink trim.

"Look, Daddy, it's all sunshine and pink," Emily said.

"That's right, it is," he replied. "You stay here with Ms. Lizzy and I'll be back in a jiffy."

A moment later he entered the shop. It was a charming place with ice cream–parlor glass-top tables and chairs in pink-and-white stripes. In fact, the main color inside was pink, and he could easily imagine him bringing Emily and Lizzy here when the place officially opened up again and the glass display case was full of goodies.

"Hi, you must be Clint Kincaid." An attractive brunette greeted him with a wide smile from behind the empty glass display case.

"That's right, and you must be Harper."

"That would be right," she replied with another smile. "I've got your order all ready to go in the back. Let me just grab it for you." She disappeared through a doorway and came back out a moment later, carrying a white cake box.

She opened the lid so he could get a look at what was inside. "It's absolutely perfect," he said. The cake was chocolate with a bright pink frosting. HAPPY BIRTHDAY EMILY was written in purple, Emily's second favorite color. On one side there was also a trio of little golden crowns.

"I told you to make it fit for a princess, and you have definitely succeeded," he said.

"I'm so glad you like it, and more importantly, I hope the birthday girl likes it as well," Harper said as she closed up the box.

"She's going to love it. It's pink and she loves all things pink." He paid for the cake and then left the shop after promising Harper he'd be back when the place opened up for full service.

He placed the confection in the back seat. "Can I see it?" Emily asked with excitement. "Daddy, can I see my cake?"

"Not until we get to the gazebo," he replied. He shot a warm glance at Lizzy. "I hope you like cake."

"I've never met one I didn't like," she replied.

As he drove to the center of town, they all talked about different flavors of cakes they enjoyed. Before he knew it, they had arrived at the beautiful gazebo. There were benches inside the big, peaked structure and once he parked, that's where the three of them headed.

Once they were situated, Emily sidled up next to Lizzy. "Is that a present for me?" she asked of the gift bag sitting at Lizzy's feet.

"It's for the birthday girl," Lizzy replied. "Do you know a birthday girl?"

"That's me! I'm the birthday girl. Can I open it?"

"Let's eat our cake first," Clint said.

Emily frowned. "I don't see a puppy, Daddy. I'm starting to get very nervous."

"The day is not over yet," Clint replied. "You have to be patient. Now, it's time to eat our cake."

Minutes later he'd served them all a piece. Emily ate hers quickly and then got up and began to dance to her own music in the center of the gazebo.

"How did your interviews go last Wednesday?" he asked Lizzy.

"Great, I've got two men starting work for me on Monday."

"Tell me about them," he replied.

"The first one is Rory O'Conner. He worked for the Mason ranch before the Masons picked up and left the area. He's a good man who has a nice family. He's married and has two small children. The other guy is new to Millsville and to me. His name is Tristen McNight. He came with good references from the Topeka area and so I decided to give him a chance."

"What brought him to Millsville from Topeka?" he asked curiously.

"According to him, an internet romance that went bad after he moved here for her."

"Ah, that stinks. And what about the third candidate?" he asked.

"Reggie Sanderson. He's another good guy and a more than competent farm hand. I just didn't need more than two."

"Would you mind if I contacted Reggie to see if he wants to come to work for me?" he asked.

"Not at all. Like I said, he's a good guy and a hard worker. I'll give you his contact information when I get home." She paused and took a bite of her cake.

A little bit of the pink frosting clung to her upper

lip. He so wanted to lean over and kiss it off. He wanted so badly to take her in his arms and lick off that errant piece of pink sugar.

It was in that moment that he realized he wouldn't be satisfied until he took Lizzy to bed.

Chapter 7

Clint awoke to the faint sound of puppy cries. Emily had been over the moon when they'd finally gotten to Gladys's place the night before and she got to pick out a puppy. They were now the proud owners of a black, long-haired toy Chihuahua named Fifi. And it sounded like Fifi was ready to get out of her crate.

He got up and dressed and then crept into Emily's bedroom, where the crate was located at the foot of Emily's bed. Emily was still asleep, but Fifi wiggled with excitement as she saw him.

He got the leash from the top of the cage, opened the cage door and then picked up the happy puppy. He clipped on the leash as he hurried toward the front door.

He stepped out into the early morning air and set Fifi on the ground. The little black dog nearly disappeared in the tall grass, reminding Clint that it was time to mow again.

As he waited for Fifi to do her business, he looked over at Lizzy's place. He'd thought he would never, ever fall in love again. He'd certainly never wanted to love again.

No matter how much a part of him thought getting too close to Lizzy was too dangerous, there was a bigger part of him that was beginning to believe he could handle it. He could keep his cover. She never needed to know about his true past. That wasn't going to be a part of his future.

He'd kissed her again last night. Even though the kiss had been short, it had definitely been hot and left him wanting more…so much more.

Fifi did what she was supposed to do and after praising her, he picked her up and carried her back into the house. He'd known when he'd bought the dog that, ultimately, he would be the one responsible for seeing to her. However, Emily would take care of the pup whenever she could. It was a good way to teach her about responsibility.

He went into the kitchen and set the dog on the floor where she danced around his feet as he made his coffee. He then shook out a bit of kibble in Fifi's new pink bowl. With her happily chowing down, he sat at the kitchen table and took a tentative sip of the hot brew.

Along with the excitement of the dog, Emily had been thrilled to receive two fashion dolls and several outfits for them from Lizzy. All in all, she'd had a great birthday and he'd enjoyed his time with his beautiful neighbor.

Lizzy had texted him the information for Reggie Sanderson the night before. Once it got a little later, he'd contact the man and set up an interview with him, if he was still available and hadn't already picked up another job.

Working in the barn, Clint had found several items he knew nothing about, making it clear to him that he needed somebody more experienced than him to help walk him through things as he went forward.

Once Fifi had eaten, he took the puppy back outside again and then carried her back to Emily's room. He placed her back in the crate where she promptly curled up and fell asleep.

Clint went into his room and got into the shower. As the warm water sluiced over him, he found himself thinking about his wife. There was a part of him that would always love her.

He and Samantha had met in a coffee shop and it had basically been love at first sight. He'd been twenty-nine and she'd been twenty-seven. They'd dated for a year and then had gotten married. She got pregnant quickly and then Emily had been born.

Samantha had been a loving wife and a wonderful mother and it had all exploded apart on that night of blood and death. He'd mourned her deeply, but his life had been empty for what felt like forever.

Sure, Emily filled a lot of his time, but the hours after Emily went to bed and the time Clint called it a night, were long quiet hours where he longed for somebody to talk to, to share with. He'd realized over the past three years that he really wasn't a man who was good all alone.

Then there were the times when he crawled into his big bed. He longed to wrap his arms around somebody, to whisper secrets and sweet things with another person. And the person he wanted was Lizzy. He was perilously close to being in love with her, and that both excited him and scared him.

He released a deep sigh and got out of the shower. It took him only minutes to dress in a clean pair of jeans and a T-shirt and then he returned to the kitchen and the coffee that still remained in his cup.

It was just after eight when he called Reggie Sanderson and set up an interview with him for later that morning. By the time he hung up, Emily had come into the kitchen. Her hair was a tousled mess and she was still in her pajamas. She held the wiggly puppy in her arms and had a huge smile on her face.

Fifi bathed her lower chin in puppy kisses. "Look, Daddy…she loves me," Emily said amid giggles. "She really loves me a lot." Clint definitely loved to hear his daughter giggle.

"She does, and what you need to do right now is, since she just woke up, you need to take her outside to go potty. I'll go get her leash and then you lead her there."

"'Kay."

Clint got the leash, and as Emily took the puppy out the front, he stood at the door and watched her. The puppy danced around, fighting against the leash, but Emily held tight and finally Fifi settled down and peed.

Minutes later Emily played with the puppy on the kitchen floor while Clint made pancakes for breakfast. "Do you think Fifi likes pancakes?" Emily asked.

"No, it's very important that you never feed Fifi people food. That could make her really sick. She has her own food, and that's all she should ever eat," he replied.

Clint continued to give his daughter doggie directions as they ate their breakfast. Fifi danced around the table and then plopped down and fell asleep once again at Emily's feet.

After breakfast, Emily, along with Fifi, went back to her bedroom to get dressed for the day and then she brought her new fashion dolls and clothes out into the living room to play, with Fifi jumping around her.

As she played and laughed at Fifi's antics, Clint cleaned up the dishes and got ready for his interview with Reggie. Once the table was clean, Clint got a piece of paper and pen out of the kitchen desk in the corner and then began to write down questions he wanted to ask the potential new hire.

At precisely eleven o'clock, a knock fell on his

door. At least Reggie Sanderson was punctual. Clint looked outside the peephole before opening the door.

"Reggie?" he asked of the tall, lean, brown-haired man who swept a battered black cowboy hat off his head.

He nodded. "And you must be Mr. Kincaid."

"Please, make it Clint. Come on in," Clint said and opened the door wider to allow the man to enter.

"And this is my daughter, Emily," Clint said. "And her brand-new puppy, Fifi."

"That's a mighty fine-looking doggie you have there, Ms. Emily," Reggie said.

"Thank you," Emily replied shyly. "She loves me a lot," she added.

"That's good," Reggie replied. "It's always nice to have a puppy who loves you."

"Why don't we go on into the kitchen," Clint said and led the way. "Can I offer you something to drink? Maybe some coffee or a soda?"

"I wouldn't turn up my nose at a cup of coffee," he replied.

Clint poured them each a mug and then joined the man at the table. Reggie Sanderson was a good-looking guy who appeared to be in his late thirties. He had the broad shoulders and worn hands of a hard worker.

"As I told you earlier on the phone, you were re-ferred to me by Lizzy Maxwell. She told me you were a good, reliable ranch hand and I definitely need somebody to help me out around this place."

"I appreciate her nice words. I brought some additional referrals, too. One is a work referral and there are also two character references." He pulled a folded sheet of paper out of his shirt pocket and handed it to Clint.

"What happened with your last job?" Clint asked curiously.

Reggie frowned. "I worked for Todd and Krista Layton for ten years...watched their kids grow up and considered them my family. Unfortunately, they fell on hard times, and a month ago, Todd had to let me go. That's the work reference I brought."

"That must have been tough on you," Clint said, seeing the emotion in the man's brown eyes.

"It was." Reggie released a deep sigh. "They were like family, but business is business, and that was then and this is now, and I'm in the market for a new job."

For the next hour the two men talked. Clint confessed that there were many things about farming that he didn't know. He was pleased that Reggie seemed extremely knowledgeable, was well-spoken and seemed eager to get back to work.

They spoke about salary and hours, and by the end of the time, Clint offered the man the job. Reggie would start on Monday, and with everything settled, Clint walked him out.

With Emily still playing in the living room, Clint returned to the kitchen table and looked over Reggie's references.

He entered the number for Todd Layton into his

cell phone, realizing he probably should have talked to Reggie's former boss before actually offering Reggie the job.

Thankfully Layton told Clint that Reggie was a hard worker and trustworthy and that he'd hated like hell to let the man go. By the time Clint got off the phone, he was confident that he'd made the right decision in hiring Reggie.

He made macaroni and cheese and cut up apple slices for lunch for Emily and then he made himself a sandwich. "Once we finish eating, there are a few things I want to do in the barn. So you can bring Fifi on the leash and we'll introduce her to the barn."

"That will be fun," Emily agreed eagerly. "Can I take Amy and Lisa, too?"

Clint frowned. "Who are Amy and Lisa?"

"My new dolls that Ms. Lizzy bought me," Emily replied as if Clint was stupid.

"Well, duh," Clint said and hit his forehead with his palm. Emily dissolved into a new set of giggles at his antics.

He wished Lizzy was here with them right now. He wished she was here sharing their laughter. What was wrong with him? He couldn't seem to get his beautiful neighbor out of his mind.

Maybe a little work in the barn would remedy that. He cleaned up from lunch and then the three of them left the house. The air had more than a hint of autumn in it. It was cooler than it had been the day before, and for the first time, he noticed that the leaves on the trees had turned beautiful colors.

Fifi continued to fight the leash as they walked toward the barn. "Why does she do that, Daddy?"

"She has to get used to the leash, bug. With enough time, she'll stop pulling like that and she'll just walk along beside you."

Emily stopped walking and picked the puppy up in her arms. "It's okay, Fifi. I'll just carry you."

"Sooner or later, you need to let her walk so she'll get used to the leash," Clint replied.

"'Kay, but just not now. She told me she wants me to carry her for today."

The puppy was going to be spoiled to death, he thought in amusement. When Clint had initially thought about getting a dog, he'd had more of a golden retriever or a German shepherd in mind. But he had to admit that Fifi, who was no bigger than a minute, was quickly getting into his heart with her loving, funny antics.

When they reached the barn, he pulled out a blanket he kept there and spread it out on the ground. Emily plopped down in the center of it and set Fifi next to her. She then pulled out her fashion dolls and began to play.

There were several horse stalls in the barn, although he housed his horse in the small stable that was on the property. However, one of the stalls in here had a shelving unit as well.

What he wanted to accomplish today was to write

down the names of all the items on the shelves that he didn't know. He would then do an internet search on them, and if he couldn't figure things out that way, then he'd ask Reggie about them on Monday morning.

He decided to start with the shelves in the stall. With Emily's chatter filling the air, he went to the back of the barn where the stall was located.

He rounded the corner and then froze. What the hell? There was an obvious depression in the hay there…as if somebody had slept there or, at the very least, had stretched out there for a while.

Blood rose up and pounded in his head. His muscles all tensed. Who had been in his barn, and why? Had it simply been a vagrant who had taken advantage of the unlocked barn doors?

Or was it possible his past was about to collide with his present?

Lizzy checked the twenty boxes that were ready to go out to the people in need in the town, making sure they all had a loaf of bread in them, among the other items.

"I think these are all good to go," she said to Elijah Simpson, the old man who ran the small food bank out of his basement.

"I always appreciate your help, Lizzy," he replied with a wide smile that showcased his white teeth against his dark skin. His smile lasted only a minute and then fell away. "It pains me that each week we seem to have more people showing up."

"Times are tough for a lot of people right now," she replied. It was a Thursday night, and the good thing that had happened that day was, at the city council meeting earlier both Butch and Letta Lee had cut their budgets to a point where Lizzy had felt good voting yes.

Elijah's basement held shelves of canned goods, boxes of a variety of pastas and canned meats. The breads that came in as donations were immediately dispersed, along with any goodies that Harper donated from her bakery.

"The work surely goes faster when there are four hands instead of just two," Elijah said.

"I always look forward to helping you out each week," she replied. She checked her wristwatch. Within ten minutes cars would begin to arrive to pick up the boxes of free food.

There were no checks into the financial needs of the people Elijah served. This was done strictly on an honor basis, and Lizzy knew most of the folks who showed up here would rather be anywhere else.

While they waited for the cars to arrive, they visited about a variety of things. Elijah was definitely one of the good people in town. He was always ready to help out people any way he could. He was a well-loved person among everyone.

Two hours later she was on her way back home. They had handed out fourteen boxes, two more than the week before. Lizzy was one of the lucky ones.

This year her crops had thrived and she'd gotten top price for the cattle she'd sold.

But she was always aware that disaster was only a breath away. There were so many variables in farming…bad weather, an insect invasion or disease could wipe out an entire year's profits.

However, none of that was on her mind for long. She had something else to look forward to…another date with Clint the next night.

She was more than a little crazy over him. She'd now spent a lot of time with him and nothing about him had turned her off. She believed he might be the one. She could easily imagine him and Emily in her life full-time. This thought nearly stole her breath away with happiness.

She was almost afraid to believe that she could have the kind of love she'd yearned for, a love that would only deepen and grow through the years. She was afraid that Clint was too good to be true. But oh, she wanted him to be the man she thought him to be.

It was an early bedtime for her. Between the city council meeting and then helping out Elijah on top of all the daily chores, she was exhausted.

The two new hires were working out great. For the last four days she'd been showing them what she expected from them and how she liked things done. They were both punctual and respectful and were hard workers.

Clint had told her he was also pleased with Reggie Sanderson working on his ranch. With charming honesty, he'd told her that Reggie was educating him about things every day.

Although she hadn't seen Clint all week, he'd called her every night and she had come to look forward to those calls. Tonight was no different. She had just gotten into bed when her phone rang and the caller identification told her it was Clint.

"How was your day?" he asked after they had greeted each other.

"Busy and I'm exhausted," she replied.

"Are we still on for tomorrow night?"

"As far as I'm concerned." The plan was for the two of them to go back to the Farmer's Club.

"Great, and since you're tired, I won't keep you. I'll just see you at seven tomorrow night," he said.

"Sounds good," she replied. Minutes later as she stared up at her darkened bedroom ceiling, a warmth filled her entire body. She loved having Clint's voice be the last thing she heard before falling asleep. The only thing that would make it better was if she heard his good-night in person with his arms wrapped around her.

The next day passed quickly and at seven, she flew out her front door to get into Clint's truck. The scent of him wrapped around her as she smiled at him.

"You look absolutely gorgeous as always," he said in greeting.

"Thank you, sir," she replied. "And you look quite nice, too." It was true. He looked sexy and fine in a black polo shirt and a pair of jeans. Nobody wore a pair of jeans as well as Clint Kincaid did.

Her nerves tingled through her veins and her body warmed, just sitting next to him. She wanted him. She couldn't remember ever wanting a man like she did him. She wanted to get physically intimate with him. Her desire for Clint had been building and building since the very first time they'd met.

They small-talked on the way into town. "Did you ever figure out who had used your barn?" she asked.

"No, and they haven't been back since. I figure maybe it was just some vagrant who needed a place to sleep for the night," he replied.

"Thankfully we haven't really had a problem with homeless people in Millsville, but I'm sure there are a few around."

They talked about the homelessness crisis in some of the bigger cities, and by that time, they were at the Farmer's Club.

There were a lot of the old-timers sitting at the bar tonight, and Lizzy greeted them and then introduced Clint to each one of them. She knew it was important for Clint to get to know the people in the community and for them to get to know him.

They made their way to an empty booth and settled in. "You can learn a lot by hanging out at the bar and talking to those men. They've seen it all when it comes to farming and they all have a lot of wisdom."

"I'll remember that, but thankfully Reggie is more

"One Minute" Survey

You get up to **FOUR books** <u>and</u> a Mystery Gift...

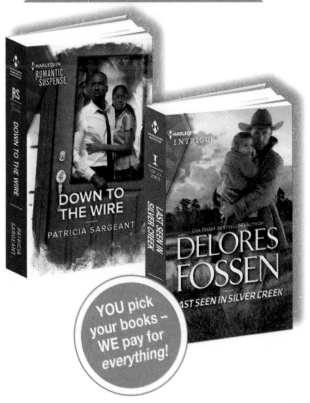

Dear Reader,

Your opinions are important to us. So if you'll participate in our fast and free "One Minute" Survey, YOU can pick up to four wonderful books that WE pay for when you try the Harlequin Reader Service!

As a leading publisher of women's fiction, we'd love to hear from you. That's why we promise to reward you for completing our survey.

IMPORTANT: Please complete the survey and return it. We'll send your Free Books and a Free Mystery Gift right away. And we pay for shipping and handling too! *We pay for EVERYTHING!*

Try **Harlequin® Romantic Suspense** and get 2 books featuring heart-racing page-turners with unexpected plot twists and irresistible chemistry that will keep you guessing to the very end.

Try **Harlequin Intrigue® Larger-Print** and get 2 books featuring action-packed stories that will keep you on the edge of your seat. Solve the crime and deliver justice at all costs.

Or TRY BOTH!

Thank you again for participating in our "One Minute" Survey. It really takes just a minute (or less) to complete the survey… and your free books and gift will be well worth it!

If you continue with your subscription, you can look forward to curated monthly shipments of brand-new books from your selected series, always at a discount off the cover price! Plus you can cancel any time. So don't miss out, return your One Minute Survey today to get your Free books.

Pam Powers

"One Minute" Survey

GET YOUR FREE BOOKS AND A FREE GIFT!

✓ Complete this Survey   ✓ Return this survey

1 Do you try to find time to read every day?

☐ YES   ☐ NO

2 Do you prefer stories with suspenseful storylines?

☐ YES   ☐ NO

3 Do you enjoy having books delivered to your home?

☐ YES   ☐ NO

4 Do you share your favorite books with friends?

☐ YES   ☐ NO

YES!

I have completed the above "One Minute" Survey. Please send me my Free Books and a Free Mystery Gift (worth over $20 retail). I understand that I am under no obligation to buy anything, as explained on the back of this card.

☐ **Harlequin® Romantic Suspense**
240/340 CTI G2AD

☐ **Harlequin Intrigue® Larger-Print**
199/399 CTI G2AD

☐ **BOTH**
240/340 & 199/399
CTI G2AE

FIRST NAME   LAST NAME

ADDRESS

APT.#   CITY

STATE/PROV.   ZIP/POSTAL CODE

EMAIL ☐ Please check this box if you would like to receive newsletters and promotional emails from Harlequin Enterprises ULC and its affiliates. You can unsubscribe anytime.

HI/HRS-1123-OM

knowledgeable than me and he's been very patient in teaching me what I need to know."

"I'm so glad he's working out for you. He's one of the good guys," she replied.

The conversation was interrupted as Ranger came to take their drink orders. She ordered a strawberry daiquiri and he ordered a scotch on the rocks.

"How are your hired help working out?" he asked once Ranger had delivered their drinks.

"Good. I'm happy with the way things are going with them," she replied. "And now that the budget has been approved for the town and I have the ranch hands I need, there should be no more drama in my life."

"No drama is a very good thing," he replied with a laugh.

The conversation between them continued to flow effortlessly and his gaze was full of warmth as it lingered on her. Of all the nights she had spent with him, tonight she felt as if he was seducing her with his sexy looks and sweet words.

His blue eyes were mesmerizing and she wanted to swim in their depths. Tonight, more than ever, she was acutely aware of not only his sensual lips and heated gaze but also the width of his shoulders and the strength of his arms. If he was trying to seduce her, it was certainly working.

When they finished up their first drink, he didn't order a second and instead had another idea. "Why don't you come back to my house for a nightcap?"

Her breath caught in the back of her throat as his

eyes filled with a heat…a simmering fire she'd never seen there before. She wanted that fire. She wanted to burn in his fire. "That sounds good to me," she replied as a new excitement sizzled through her veins.

They left the bar, and on the ride back to his place, they were both relatively quiet, but she felt the heightened sexual tension snapping in the air between them.

She tried to calm her nerves. Maybe he really just wanted a nightcap with her. After all, Emily was in the house. How hot could things really get?

When they reached his place, he grabbed her hand as they walked up to the front door. When they entered the house, Rosa was there to greet them.

Lizzy had always liked the widow, who was cheerful and kind whenever Lizzy met her someplace in town. Tonight, was no different. She greeted Lizzy with her bright smile.

"How are you doing, Lizzy?" she asked.

"I'm getting by," Lizzy replied. "How about you?"

"When you get to be my age, you're just happy to wake up each morning," the older woman replied and then turned to Clint. "She's sound asleep. And the puppy is in the crate, sleeping as well."

"Thank you, Rosa, for staying late this evening. I'll walk you out to your car." He turned to Lizzy. "Why don't you just make yourself comfortable in the living room and I'll be right back."

She nodded and headed into the living room. She sat on the sofa to wait for Clint, and a few minutes later, he entered the room. "Now, what would you like to drink? I've got vodka, whiskey and scotch, along with soda."

"I'll take a Coke with a small splash of whiskey," she replied. "And make sure it's just a small splash."

"Got it. I'll be right back again." He left the room to go into the kitchen.

A few minutes later he returned with the drinks in hand. He held one out to her and then sank down next to her on the sofa, with his own.

"Cheers," he said and they clinked their glasses together and then they both took a drink.

"Hmm, you got it just right," she said and put her glass down on a coaster on the coffee table.

"Good." He set his glass down also and gazed at her intently. "Lizzy, you've been such an unexpected joy in my life. I can't tell you how much I look forward to seeing you, to spending time with you."

"I feel the same way about you," she confessed and felt the warmth of a blush creeping onto her cheeks.

He moved closer to her, and her heartbeat accelerated. "All I've been able to think about all evening is how much I want to kiss you again."

"Then by all means, kiss me."

He gathered her into his arms and his lips met hers. He tasted of the faint bite of scotch and sweet, hot desire. As he deepened the kiss with his tongue, she wrapped her arms around his neck and leaned closer to him.

The kiss continued until she was half-breathless, and then his lips slid down her throat with nipping kisses that only enflamed and heightened her desire for him.

He moaned, letting her know he desired her, too. She threw back her head to allow him better access to her throat as his kisses continued. He sparked fire wherever his lips touched and when he finished with her throat his lips reclaimed hers in a fiery kiss. He finally pulled his mouth from hers and instead gazed at her with a hunger that stole the rest of her breath away.

He reached up and moved an errant strand of her hair away from her cheek. "I want you, Lizzy. I don't just want to kiss you. I want to feel your naked body next to mine. I want to make love to you. Will you come to my bedroom and make love with me?"

"Wha—what about Emily?" she asked, still half-breathless.

"She's a sound sleeper," he replied. He stood and offered her a hand. "If you tell me no, there certainly won't be any hard feelings," he said. "But I hope you feel the same way I do. I hope you want me as much as I want you."

She stood and slipped her hand in his. "Oh, Clint, I do."

As he led her down the hallway to his bedroom, her heart beat frantically and her nipples grew erect and pressed against her bra in sweet anticipation of what was to come.

His king-size bed was covered in a plain navy blue spread, and a lamp on his nightstand was turned on, creating a soft glow of illumination in the room. He led her to the side of the bed and then pulled her into his arms and kissed her once again.

She couldn't remember wanting a man as much as she wanted Clint. It felt different than anything she'd ever experienced in her past. As he pulled her more tightly against him, she could tell he was already aroused and that excited her even more.

As the kiss continued, he stepped back from her a bit and his arms moved from the back of her to the front. His hands cupped her breasts and her nipples once again hardened as if aching for a more intimate touch.

She pushed back from him, released a deep tremulous breath, and pulled her blouse over her head and dropped it to the floor behind her. His gaze burned into hers with an intensity that was positively bewitching. In turn, he pulled off his shirt, leaving his muscled chest beautifully exposed to her.

Together they took off their shoes and socks and then took off their pants, leaving her clad in her bra and a wispy pair of red panties and him in a pair of black boxers.

He unfolded the bedspread, got in beneath the sheet and then beckoned her to join him there. She immediately slid beneath the cover and into his arms.

The skin-on-skin contact excited her as their legs wound together and his hands caressed up and down her back. He kissed her again…deep and hot, stealing her breath away once again.

Within minutes her bra was off, and she moaned with pleasure as his hands cupped her bare breasts and his thumbs rubbed across her engorged nipples.

His tongue replaced his thumbs, shooting electric currents from her breasts to the very center of her. He nipped and licked her nipples with a fiery heat. As his mouth loved her breasts, his hands slid slowly down her abdomen to the waistband of her panties.

His fingers danced back and forth across the top of her panties until she was half-mad and then he began to take them off her. She aided him by raising up so he could slide them all the way to her feet, and once there, she kicked them off.

His hand once again returned to the very center of her. This time his warm fingers moved against her in a rhythm that built up a sweet, hot, rising tension inside her.

"Clint." She was barely able to whisper his name as the mounting tide inside her rose even higher. Higher and higher she climbed, and then she was there, riding the crest of a wave that left her gasping and yet wanting more.

Clint kicked his boxers off and then crouched between her legs. His eyes blazed with a fire that immediately consumed her. She was lost in his eyes… lost in him. Before she'd even caught her breath from her orgasm, he slowly entered her.

He hissed with pleasure and she moaned as he remained unmoving. He completely filled her up. "Lizzy, you feel so good," he whispered next to her ear.

"Oh, so do you," she replied breathlessly. Her hands swept up and down his back, loving the feel of his warm skin and the underlying play of his muscles.

She gasped as he began to stroke in and out of her. He moved slowly at first…long, smooth strokes that caused her pleasure to once again climb higher and higher.

She stopped caressing his back and instead held tight to his shoulders as he increased his pace. Electricity snapped and sizzled in her veins and she was half-mindless as she felt the imminence of another rising climax.

When it finally washed over her again, she whispered his name over and over again. Then he was there with her, moaning deep in the back of his throat as he found his own release.

For several long moments they remained locked together, their breaths slowly finding a more normal rhythm. He finally rolled away from her a bit.

He reached out and brushed a strand of her hair away from her face. "That went by way too fast, but despite that, it was absolutely amazing." His gaze was soft and warm on her.

"I thought it was amazing, too," she replied. It had been more than amazing, it had been positively earth-shattering. He'd taken her to a place she'd never been before, to a height of physical and emotional feelings that felt new and wonderful.

He frowned suddenly. "Everything happened so quickly, we didn't even use any protection. I just want you to know that it's been over three years since I've been with anyone and I'm clean."

"I'm clean, too…and I'm on the pill, so we're good," she assured him.

His frown disappeared and he leaned forward and gave her a soft, sweet kiss. "Stay with me tonight?" he asked.

Her heart beat a little faster at his request. She would love to stay here and sleep in his arms. She would also like to wake up with him in the morning.

"I'll cook breakfast," he said as if to entice her into agreeing.

"I thought you couldn't cook," she replied.

He grinned. "Breakfast, I can do."

Their voices were soft whispers, so intimate in the semidarkness of the room. She suddenly thought of something. "How were you planning on taking me home tonight since Rosa is gone and Emily is asleep?"

He smiled at her sheepishly. "To be honest, I hadn't thought that far ahead. I just knew I wanted to hold you in my arms through the night."

"Well, you're a lucky man because I would like that, too. Could you loan me one of your T-shirts to sleep in?"

"That can be arranged."

They both got out of the bed and he opened a drawer and handed her the makeshift nightwear. She then went into the adjoining bathroom while he went into the bathroom in the hallway.

She pulled the T-shirt over her head and then stared at her reflection in the mirror. Her cheeks were flushed and her eyes held the shine of a satisfied woman. She was happy and eager now to cuddle and sleep with him.

Minutes later she was back in his bed. He turned out the lamp and she snuggled into his arms. With his arms wrapped around her, she felt safe and secure.

"Comfortable?" his voice was a soft whisper.

"Very," she replied.

"I love having you here in my bed."

She smiled into the darkness. "I love being here."

"Are you sleepy?" he asked.

"I could sleep," she replied.

"Then, good night, sweet Lizzy."

"Good night, my sweet Clint."

She'd already believed she was on the verge of being in love with Clint. She was close enough to him that she believed she could hear his heartbeat. The scent of him eddied around her. His arms were so warm and strong around her, and in that moment, she realized she wasn't just on the verge of falling in love… She was madly and crazy in love with her neighbor.

Chapter 8

Clint awoke just after six the next morning. Lizzy slept soundly next to him, and for a moment, he just gazed at her. In the faint sunlight that crept through the window, she appeared to be sprinkled with gold and looked as beautiful as he'd ever seen her. Her long eyelashes dusted her upper cheeks and a half smile played on her lips, as if her dreams were happy ones.

They had made love for a second time in the middle of the night. It had been much slower and more intense, and when it was over, the words *I love you* had trembled on his lips.

Thankfully he'd managed to catch himself and hadn't said those words aloud, but he'd felt them trembling deep in his heart. Before he spoke those words to Lizzy, he had to make sure he wasn't confusing physical attraction with love. And there was no question that he felt a strong physical attraction to Lizzy.

He slid out of the bed, grateful that he didn't wake her. He grabbed his boxers and jeans and then went into the hallway bathroom. He pulled on his pants, deciding he'd shower later, after he took Lizzy home. He brushed his teeth with the extra toothbrush he kept there and sprayed himself with his spare bottle of cologne.

He then hurried into the kitchen. Right now, he wanted to get some bacon frying before Lizzy or Emily woke up. On the way to the kitchen, he peeked into Emily's bedroom. Thankfully not only was Emily still sleeping soundly but Fifi was still asleep, too.

Once in the kitchen he started a pot of coffee and then got the bacon into the skillet. Minutes later the scent of the frying bacon filled the air and he poured himself a cup of the freshly brewed coffee.

He sank down at the table and his thoughts returned to the night before. Actually, making love with Lizzy had not only lived up to all the fantasies he'd had of her prior but it had surpassed all of his fantasies. She'd been sexy and hot and giving all at the same time.

Even now, despite the night of lovemaking, he wanted her again. He had a feeling he could make love to her a million times and it would never be enough for him.

Was he simply physically attracted to her? He

thought of the deep conversations he'd had with her and the laughter they had shared. No, he realized his attraction to her went much further than the strong physical draw he felt toward her.

At that moment Lizzy came into the kitchen. She was clad in the clothes she'd worn the night before and wore a bright smile. "There's nothing better than waking up to the smell of a man cooking you bacon," she said.

He laughed. "Does that happen a lot in your life?" He gestured her to the kitchen table.

"It's happened exactly once... This morning," she said with one of her grins.

He laughed again and poured her a cup of coffee. "Did you sleep well?" he asked as he carried her cup to the table.

"Once I fell asleep for good, I slept like the dead," she replied. "But a naughty man woke me in the middle of the night."

"Ha, I could have sworn a naughty woman woke me in the middle of the night," he replied. They both laughed.

He walked back over to the stove and then turned back to look at her. "Any regrets?"

"Absolutely none," she replied. "As far as I'm concerned, it was a wonderful night and I would do it all over again in a hot minute."

"Don't tempt me," he said with a laugh. "It was a wonderful night," he agreed. He began to flip the bacon strips. As he worked to make breakfast, they talked about some of the people she had introduced him to the night before.

It felt intimate, to be sharing the kitchen as the sun rose outside. He remembered how much he'd always enjoyed being in the kitchen in the mornings with his wife.

Samantha had been a morning person. But sadly, she was gone now and forever and he was definitely enjoying this time quiet "kitchen time" with Lizzy.

Their conversation jarred to a halt when Emily's squeal pierced the air. "Ms. Lizzy, you're here," she exclaimed with excitement. "And it's morning time."

Lizzy laughed and got up from her chair to greet her. "I am here, and not only do you look cute as a bug in your pink pajamas but Fifi looks very happy, too."

"She loves me," Emily replied. As if to prove her point, Fifi lavished kisses on the underside of Emily's chin.

"She'll love you even more if you take her outside for her morning duties," Clint said and moved his skillet off the burner. "Go get her leash and I'll walk out with you."

"I can go with Emily," Lizzy said.

"I want Ms. Lizzy to go with me," Emily replied.

Clint rolled his eyes. "So, you're just throwing me to the curb like an old shoe," he replied.

"Oh, Daddy. You're not an old shoe, but Ms. Lizzy is better today," Emily replied with a giggle.

"Yes, I'm better today, Daddy," Lizzy said with a wide grin at him. "So where is Fifi's leash?"

"In my bedroom. Come on, Ms. Lizzy." Emily grabbed her hand. "You can see my room. It's all pink."

"Pink is my favorite color," Lizzy said.

"Me, too," Emily replied with excitement.

As the two females left the kitchen, Clint moved his skillet back to the burner. He grabbed the package of frozen hash browns from the freezer and dumped the contents into the pan.

He was going all out for breakfast this morning in honor of Lizzy being a guest. Besides, he'd always liked a good hearty breakfast to start the day. He heard the front door open and knew Lizzy and Emily had taken Fifi outside.

It did his heart good that Lizzy was so open and loving to Emily. That only made him like Lizzy more.

About ten minutes passed and then Lizzy and Emily came giggling back into the kitchen. "What's so funny?" he asked them.

"Nothing…just girl talk," Lizzy replied airily.

"Yeah, just girl talk, Daddy," Emily echoed with another giggle. "Can I unhook Fifi now?" she asked.

"Unhook her but take the leash right back to where it belongs," Clint said.

"'Kay." Emily unfastened the dog and then raced back to her bedroom to put the leash on top of the crate.

"So how are things going with the new puppy?" Lizzy asked.

"Fairly good. She's had a few mistakes in the house,

but I expected that to happen. It was more human error than puppy error."

"Is Emily pulling her own weight?"

"For the most part. We'll see what happens when the novelty of it wears off. Now, I have a very important question for you… Do you like your eggs fried or is scrambled your preference?"

Within another ten minutes they were all seated at the table enjoying the breakfast of bacon, hash browns, scrambled eggs and toast.

As Emily chattered to Lizzy, Clint just sat back and enjoyed the sound of their conversation. This felt good. It seemed so right. It felt like the warmth of family and he'd been missing this feeling forever.

Emily's utter happiness shone on her little features and in the brightness of the blue of her eyes as she talked with Lizzy. He wanted this for her… He wanted her to have a woman in her life who she could admire and love. He wanted her to have the warmth of a complete family surrounding her as she grew up.

Was he ready for this now? Was it even possible that he could have all of it with the secrets that darkened his past? That could possibly intrude into his present? He just wasn't sure.

Right now, he was just enjoying his time with Lizzy. He was trying not to think about the future too much. He was still a bit hesitant to bring Lizzy fully into his life, and yet the idea of not ever seeing her again broke his heart. God, he was so confused about his life and her. Right now, it seemed best to just take it day by day and not think too much about the future.

Still, after what they had shared last night, he couldn't imagine not having her in his life. Aside from the fact that their conversations were wonderfully easy and they laughed together often, she had been an amazing lover.

She'd been eager and giving and she'd stoked a fire in him that had been beyond incredible. The first time they'd made love, she had him so excited that things had happened very fast. The second time he'd had more control and things had lasted longer.

Right now, seated at the kitchen table, he found himself wanting her all over again.

All too soon, breakfast was over and it was time to take Lizzy home. Emily put Fifi back in her crate and then got dressed for the day, while Clint and Lizzy cleaned up the mealtime mess.

"I have to admit, you make a fine breakfast, Mr. Kincaid," Lizzy said.

"Thanks, I like a good one before starting the day," he replied.

They finished the cleanup, and finally, they were all in the truck. "Can you be at my house tomorrow morning when I wake up, Ms. Lizzy? Daddy could make you pancakes," Emily said as Clint started the engine. "He makes really good pancakes."

"I'm sorry, Emily, but I can't. At least we had fun this morning, right?" Lizzy replied.

"Right," Emily agreed, although her tone was

mournful. "But I want you to be at my house every morning. Daddy, why can't you just marry Ms. Lizzy and then she'd be my new mommy and be at our house all the time. That would make me so happy."

Clint's stomach muscles tightened as his brain scrambled to find a reasonable answer.

"It's not as easy as that," Lizzy replied. "Right now, your daddy and I are good friends, but we're not in a position to get married."

"That's sad because I love you so much, Ms. Lizzy," Emily replied mournfully.

"I love you, too, Emily," Lizzy replied. "And we'll keep seeing each other and spending time with each other whenever we can, okay?"

"'Kay," Emily replied, but it was obvious she wasn't happy with the situation.

A few moments later they pulled up in front of Lizzy's house. Clint got out of the truck to walk her to her door. "Thanks for last night," she said once they were there.

"Thank you," he replied. "Lizzy, it was a wonderful night," he said warmly.

"It was," she agreed with one of her beautiful smiles.

"I'll call you later."

"Okay."

He leaned forward and quickly kissed her on the forehead, then they said their goodbyes and he hurried back to his truck.

"How about when we get home, we go out to the barn and you can play there?" He was still cataloging all the bottles and ointments that were stored inside, and besides, Emily always liked playing in the barn.

"Can I bring two baby dolls with me?"

"I think we can manage that," Clint replied.

It was about fifteen minutes later that the two were traipsing through the grass, toward the barn in the distance. He held on to Fifi's leash while Emily's arms were filled with two of her favorite dolls.

Thankfully kids didn't hold on to sadness for too long. Although Emily had been sad that Lizzy wouldn't be in their kitchen the next morning, she now sang a happy song as they walked into the barn.

He unhooked Fifi and then put the blanket down on the ground so Emily could play. Fifi jumped and ran around her, making Emily giggle over and over again at the doggie's antics.

Clint wasn't sure his life could get any better than it was at this very moment. His daughter was healthy and happy, he was learning his way around the farm and he had a very hot neighbor who had not only been a good friend but now had become his lover as well.

With Emily playing happily, Clint headed to the back stall with its shelves. He was determined today to finish cataloguing what was on the shelves. He carried with him a notepad and a pen. He rounded the corner and then froze in his tracks. The notepad and pen fell from his hands as he stared at what was on the hay in the stall.

Five dead blackbirds formed a circle there. What

the hell? He backed out of the stall, his heart beating frantically. There was no way those birds accidently flew into the barn, died and then arranged themselves in a circle. Somebody had done this. But who? What did it mean? Who had done this and why?

Lizzy had just gotten out of the shower and was half-dressed when her phone rang and she saw it was Clint. She frowned. Why would he be calling her so soon after dropping her off? She knew he intended to work in his barn after returning home.

"Clint?" she answered.

"Uh, Lizzy, I'm sorry to ask this, but could you come over here and watch Emily for a little while so I can speak with Chief Calloway out in my barn?"

She could hear the thick stress in his voice. And why did he need the police in his barn? A dozen questions raced through her mind, but she asked none of them, certain that she'd find out what was going on later, when she got there.

"Of course," she replied. "I'll be right over."

It only took her a few minutes to finish dressing and then get to Clint's place. Dallas wasn't there yet. Clint greeted her at the front door, a deep frown etching across his forehead. "Thanks for coming."

"Ms. Lizzy, Daddy said you could play with me for a little while," Emily said.

"That's right, honey," Lizzy replied.

"I'm going to go get my baby dolls," Emily said

and took off running toward her bedroom. Fifi ran after her, yipping with excitement.

"What's going on?" Lizzy asked softly once Emily was out of earshot.

Clint frowned once again and his eyes darkened. "I've got some dead birds in my barn."

Lizzy's concern instantly eased. "Clint, it's not common, but occasionally birds fly into a barn and into a wall and die."

He shook his head, but before he could say anything more, Dallas knocked on the door. He had Officer Benjamin Cooper with him, and while Clint greeted the two, Emily came running back into the room with two dolls in her arms.

"Let's head outside and you can fill me in as we walk," Dallas said.

The three men left the house and Lizzy sank down in the middle of the floor to play with Emily. She was the mommy doll and Emily was the daughter doll. Emily's doll would cry and Lizzy's doll would comfort her. Emily's doll would laugh and the mommy doll would laugh with her. Then, when Emily's doll was bad, mommy doll punished her by putting her in time-out.

The next forty minutes or so went by quickly. The two laughed together as the puppy raced circles around them, occasionally tumbling head over heels, and then plopped down and fell asleep at Emily's side.

It wasn't long after that when the men came back inside. "Emily, why don't you go play in your bedroom for a little while. Daddy needs some grown-up time with Ms. Lizzy and these two nice men."

"'Kay," Emily replied. She picked up her two dolls and headed for her bedroom with Fifi prancing behind her.

Lizzy was confused as she followed Clint into the kitchen where Dallas and Benjamin were already seated at the table. It was obvious this was about more than a dead bird or two in the barn. What exactly had happened and why did the men want to speak with her?

"Coffee?" Clint asked.

"I wouldn't mind a cup," Dallas replied.

"Might as well pour one for me," Lizzy said.

"Make that three," Benjamin said.

While they waited for Clint to serve the coffees, Dallas looked at Lizzy. "I wanted you here because I want to ask you a few questions."

"Okay," she replied, wondering what the big deal was about a couple of dead birds in Clint's barn.

"Do you know what's happened in the barn?" Dallas asked her.

"Not exactly. All I know is it concerns some dead birds," Lizzy replied.

"Five dead blackbirds, their bodies all arranged in a circle, to be exact," Dallas said.

A chill raced up Lizzy's back as she stared at Dallas in stunned shock. Five dead blackbirds? In folklore, a dead blackbird could mean many things and one of those meanings was death to somebody.

This was definitely far more serious than just a bird that had hit a wall in the barn. Who on earth was responsible for this? Why Clint's barn? What, exactly, did it all mean?

Everyone was served their coffee and then Clint sat down. "Have you seen any strangers hanging around Clint's barn?" Dallas asked Lizzy.

"No, nobody but Clint and Reggie Sanderson," she replied. "But honestly I don't pay that much attention to Clint's barn."

"And nothing strange in your barn?" He took a sip of his coffee, looking anything but relaxed.

"I haven't yet been out to the barn this morning," she replied. She hoped nothing had been done in her barn as well. "What do you think this is all about?" she asked the lawman.

He swept a hand through his hair and released a deep sigh. "Hell, if I know." He turned his attention to Clint. "And you're sure that nothing in your background would warrant this kind of thing."

"No, uh, nothing," Clint replied. Lizzy stared at the man she had just made love with the night before. For some reason his response sounded a little bit forced to her ears.

"Have you had any problems with somebody in town? Is there anyone who might be angry with you?" Dallas asked.

Clint shook his head. "No, nobody. I don't know that many people yet, but everyone Lizzy has introduced me to has been very pleasant and I've been nice back to them."

Dallas looked back at Lizzy. "What about you, Lizzy? I know you and Clint have been seeing each other a lot. Is there a former boyfriend who might be angry about that? Somebody who might see Clint as a romantic threat?"

"Before Clint, it had been years since I'd dated anyone seriously. So, the answer is no. There's nobody in my past that would be jealous about me seeing Clint," she replied.

Dallas released a deep sigh. "You know when I think about blackbirds, I can't help but think about cornfields. I'm just hoping this isn't some kind of a new, sick kind of game from the Scarecrow Killer," Dallas said, creating a new chill to waltz up Lizzy's back.

"If it is that, then why put the birds in Clint's barn?" Lizzy asked. "I mean, I'm obviously his type."

"Who knows why this bastard does what he does," Dallas replied in obvious frustration. He looked at Lizzy once again. "I would say it's more important than ever now, that you watch your surroundings. You are his type, and if this is his new handiwork, it might mean that he's got you in his sights even though the birds were left in Clint's barn. We need to go over to your place and check out yours."

"That's fine with me. The barn is unlocked. As far as my own safety, I'm now carrying my gun wherever I go. I do have a concealed-carry license," she replied.

Dallas frowned. "Normally I wouldn't recommend carrying, but under these circumstances, I think it might be a smart thing for you to do. I wish I could put officials at every potential victim's home, but I just don't have the available manpower to do that."

"We all understand that, Dallas," Lizzy said. "At the end of the day, we're all responsible for taking care of our own safety and security."

"I just wish I could get into this guy's head and figure him out." Dallas leaned back in his chair and released another deep sigh. "Of course, it's very possible this has nothing to do with the Scarecrow Killer."

"Then, what could it possibly be about?" Lizzy asked.

Dallas shook his head. "I wish I had some answers for you, but at this point I don't."

"Is Emily in any danger?" Clint, who had mostly been silent in the conversation, asked worriedly.

"I don't know. There's nothing that would make me think she's in danger. However, I'd keep her inside and if she does go outside, keep her close to you," Dallas said. He leaned forward and drank the last of his coffee. "Officer Cooper here has taken pictures of the scene and I'm going to get several more officers out here to search the barn and see if we can come up with something more to identify who killed those birds."

"How...how were they killed?" Lizzy asked.

"We aren't sure. There is no sign of trauma on their bodies," Benjamin said and shook his head. "It's difficult to catch one wild bird, let alone five."

Dallas stood and Benjamin followed suit. "Please stay away from the barn for the rest of the day," he instructed Clint. "My men will probably be in and out of there for most of the afternoon."

"Trust me, I'm not in a hurry to get back in there," Clint replied. Both him and Lizzy got out of their chairs and walked with the other two toward the front door.

She thought about saying something to Benjamin about Bailey, but now wasn't the right time or the place to try to play matchmaker.

"Lizzy, I forgot what you told me... Is your barn locked?" Dallas asked her.

"No, it's not," she replied.

"Then I'll send an officer or two over there to check things out."

"Thanks, I appreciate it," she replied.

Standing on the porch with the men, she thought about all those times she'd felt as if somebody was watching her and she'd written them off to paranoia.

Maybe somebody really had been studying her after all. Maybe the Scarecrow Killer had been stalking her...scrutinizing her every move. This thought renewed the chill that swept through her body.

She wished Clint would pull her into his arms. As

if he read her thoughts, he did just that. He pulled her tight against him...against his warmth.

"Are you okay?" he murmured into her ear.

"I will be," she replied.

"Want to come back in for another cup of coffee?" Clint asked her as the two lawmen went back to the barn to wait for additional officers to arrive.

"Sure," she replied.

He released his hold on her. "Go on to the kitchen, I'm just going to do a quick check on Emily," he said.

She went back in and sat down, and a few minutes later, he came into the kitchen, poured them each another cup of coffee and then he joined her at the table.

"This is all so crazy," she said.

"Tell me about it," he replied with a deep frown. "Who would even think to do something like that?"

"I can't imagine." She took a sip of her coffee and then continued, "It's hard to believe that it was only a couple of hours ago that we were all sitting here eating breakfast and laughing together."

"Yeah, how quickly things can change," he replied. He gazed at her intently. "I just want you to remember that if anything goes awry at your place, I can be over there in a matter of minutes."

"Thank you, I appreciate that." She knew he meant the words to comfort her, but the mere mention of anything "going awry" at her place caused her nerves to burn with anxiety.

"Maybe this has nothing to do with the Scarecrow Killer," he said.

"Then, what would it be about?" She gazed at him closely. "Are you sure there isn't anything at all in your past that might have something to do with this?"

His gaze shot to someplace just over her head and then he looked back at her. "No, nothing," he replied, but there were dark shadows in his eyes that made her question whether or not to believe him. "Maybe we have some Satan worshippers out there somewhere and they used my barn for some sort of a strange ritual. It sure looked like a ritual, with the birds all arranged in a circle."

"I can't imagine anyone in this town being a devil worshipper," she replied.

"Yes, but nobody in town believes one of their own is the Scarecrow Killer," he countered.

"Point taken," she replied.

It wasn't long after that when Dallas came back in to report that nothing strange was found in Lizzy's barn, which filled her with relief.

She left Clint's house soon after that and as she drove the short distance back to her place, her mind was filled with thoughts of Clint and everything that had just happened.

Five dead blackbirds. Who had done it, and of all the barns in the area, why had they been left in Clint's? And why did she feel just a little bit of doubt in Clint's reply about nothing like this ever happening before in his past?

She'd believed he was perfect for her. She not only thought of him as a best friend, but she had fallen deeply in love with him. She now realized she didn't know a lot about his past, and she found herself wondering who Clint Maxwell really was.

Chapter 9

It was just after seven on Friday night when Clint walked into the Farmer's Club alone. He'd invited Lizzy to go out with him, but she'd told him she had some paperwork she had to get done and she was having a late-night meeting with her hired help.

He knew her corn was in the process of being harvested. He'd seen a combine moving back and forth across her fields.

Jerry West was set to start on Clint's corn on Tuesday. Clint was eager to see how the process was done up close and personal.

Emily had been asked to a birthday slumber party for the night. Clint had previously met the mother and father of the birthday girl on Wednesday night when there had been a parents' night at the school.

He'd not only met them, but he'd also talked with Emily's teacher. Mrs. Barlow had spoken highly of Emily's intelligence and her wonderfully sunny personality. It had been nice to hear her glowing report about how his daughter was doing in school.

When he'd dropped Emily off at her friend's a few minutes ago, there were three giggling girls already there. Emily would have been brokenhearted if he'd told her she couldn't go, but he felt confident that Emily would be safe and well cared for throughout the night.

It had been a very long week. He felt like Lizzy had pulled back from him a bit, and while he would have liked to have her with him this evening, he really just wanted a drink and a little downtime.

He took an empty stool next to one of the old-timers, a man named Walt Schumer. He'd been introduced to the man when he and Lizzy had been in the bar previously.

Walt greeted him with a friendly smile. "Evening, Clint."

"Back at you, Walt," Clint replied.

Ranger greeted him, and Clint ordered a scotch on the rocks.

"Heard you had some trouble at your place earlier in the week," Ranger said a moment later as he delivered Clint's drink to him.

"How did you hear about it?" Clint asked curiously.

Ranger grinned at him. "It's almost been a week. By now probably everyone in town has heard about it. Gossip flies fast in this little town."

"Does Dallas have any clues as to who would do such a thing?" Walt asked.

"Not that he's shared with me," Clint replied. The police had been in his barn all day long on the day the birds had been discovered, but as far as Clint was concerned, they had come away with nothing to help identify the guilty culprit or culprits.

Clint hadn't spoken to Dallas since then. However, he'd been grateful that they'd taken the dead birds with them when they'd left at the end of that horrible day.

The next morning Clint had gone to the hardware store and had bought a sturdy lock that he'd installed on the barn doors. Nobody was going to sleep or easily walk into his barn again.

"Dead blackbirds, that's some bad stuff," Walt said with a shake of his head. Clint would guess Walt to be in his mid-eighties. He had a full head of gray hair and his skin tone was the tan of a man who spent long hours outside in the sun. From what Lizzy had told him, the man was a widower whose grown kids lived out of state.

"Tell me what it means, Walt. Lizzy told me it could mean a death coming, is that true?" Clint asked.

"That's one of the superstitions about dead blackbirds. It could also mean a change of some kind is coming."

"I definitely like that better," Clint replied ruefully.

"But aside from the superstitions, somebody obviously has it out for you," Walt said.

"Yeah, I know, but I just don't know who. You ever see anything like this before?" Clint asked the older man.

"I've seen a lot of things and I've been around these parts longer than a snake's tail, and I've never seen or heard about anything like this," Walt replied. "Could this be some kind of weird California stuff that followed you here?"

"Not that I know of." The two men fell silent and Clint took a sip of his drink, enjoying the slow slide of heat down his throat.

"I heard your corn was going to be harvested next week," Walt said.

"That's right. Jerry West is going to take care of it for me."

"Jerry's a good man and honest as the day is long," Walt replied.

"Anything important that I should know about when they work on my place?" Clint asked.

"Yeah, keep the coffee coming…hot and strong," Walt said with a twinkle in his pale blue eyes. "There's something about a combine that makes a man yearn for coffee."

"Got it, and do I need to provide a meal for the men?"

"Donuts in the morning…ham sandwiches at lunch and a nice, hearty supper would be a bonus that the men would surely appreciate. If you feed a man well, he'll remember you at the next harvesting."

"Good to know," Clint replied. He could manage the donuts and ham sandwiches, and maybe he could pick up something at the café that evening for the men.

Once again, they fell silent. The music overhead sang about a lost love and as he sipped at his drink, thoughts of Lizzy filled his head.

Had she really been too busy tonight to come out with him, or had the blackbirds scared her away from him? They had spoken on the phone to each other almost every night, and during those calls, he hadn't felt her shift away from him.

He didn't want to lose her. The depths of his feelings toward her slammed him in the center of his chest. She'd brought a lightness into his life, a light and laughter that had been missing. Before her, he'd just been existing and not really living. Before her, he'd been in a cocoon of sadness and fear and guilt.

He and Walt visited for a little while longer and then he finished his drink, and despite the fact that it was relatively early, he decided to call it a night. "Walt, it's been a pleasure but I think I'm done for." He slid off his stool and motioned to Ranger for his check.

"I enjoyed the visit," Walt replied.

"Heading out?" Ranger asked as he approached Clint.

"Yeah, I'm going home and into my easy chair," Clint replied as he paid for his drink.

"After the week you've had, I don't blame you a bit," Walt said.

"Thanks, Walt, and good night," Clint said and then headed out the door. The cool night air wrapped around him as he walked to his truck parked across the street against the curb. He'd just reached the driver's door when a shot rang out.

Almost simultaneously a bullet smashed the driver-side window and it exploded. Clint hit the ground, his heart thundering loudly in his ears.

What the hell? His brain worked to make sense of what had just happened. Somebody had just fired at him. Was the person with the gun still hiding in the shadows, waiting to get a better shot in if Clint got up from the asphalt?

He remained down as several minutes ticked by. Was the shooter still around? He hadn't even seen exactly where the bullet had come from.

At that moment a couple stepped out of the bar. "Go back inside and call the police," he shouted to them. "There's an active shooter out here."

The two people turned and hurried back into the bar. A few minutes later Dallas's car appeared, the lights on top painting all the landscape in swirling reds and blues.

He pulled up behind Clint's truck and it was only then that Clint felt safe enough to get to his feet. Dallas jumped out of his patrol car with a gun in hand.

"So, what happened? I got a call about an active shooter," he said tersely.

"I was just getting ready to get in my truck when this happened," Clint said and stepped back so Dallas could survey the damage to his window. At that moment two more patrol cars pulled up and parked. "I heard a shot and then a bullet hit it," he added.

"Did you see where the shot came from?" Dallas asked.

"No, and I can't tell you anything about the shooter. I was just reaching for my door handle when the bullet hit my window." As Clint digested how close it had come to him, his blood turned to ice. He definitely could have been killed…shot in the back.

Dallas turned to the four officers who stood behind him. "Do a thorough search of the area across the street. Be on the lookout for any casings or anything else that might pertain to this."

The officers took off, high-beam flashlights in hand. "I'd say this might be a random thing except this, on top of the blackbirds, tells me it isn't random at all. I don't know what you've said or done to somebody to get them so pissed off at you. But somebody is angry enough to try to kill you."

"I swear to God, Chief Calloway, I have no idea who this person could be," Clint replied in frustration. "I don't have any idea why this is all happening to me."

"Let me check out your truck and see if we can find a bullet. It's got to be lodged someplace inside, because it didn't exit through your passenger window. And please, make it Dallas."

"Dallas, it is." Clint stepped back so Dallas could get into the cab of the vehicle.

As Dallas crawled into the driver side of the truck to check things out, Clint stared up into the night sky, once again racking his brain to think of anyone he might have angered. There was simply nobody. He couldn't think of one single person he could have angered, especially angered enough for them to want to kill him.

What did this mean for him…for Emily? Were they going to have to pack up and move once again? Emily was so happy here. He was happy here, too. He didn't want to have to leave Lizzy and move to another place. He definitely didn't want to start over somewhere else.

Still, he didn't believe this was anyone from his past. He felt like so far this had all the earmarks of a local. But who? And why?

"Found it," Dallas said triumphantly. He came back out of the truck and held out his palm to Clint. In the center was a small, misshapen bullet. "It looks like it's a small caliber, probably from a handgun. I'll know more about it once I get it back to the station. Right now, I need to get this into an evidence bag. I'll be right back."

He walked around to the back of his patrol car and opened his trunk. He pulled out a small brown envelope and dropped the bullet into it and then walked back around to where Clint still stood.

"You were a very lucky man tonight," Dallas said. "If that bullet had strayed a little bit to the left, you would have been shot in the back. Or maybe somebody is just warning you."

"Warning me about what?" Clint sighed in even more frustration. "I'm hoping you and your men will find something that might identify this guy."

"We'll keep looking. In the meantime, you're free to go. I'll contact you if I need anything else from you," Dallas said. "And while you're out and about... watch your back."

"Thanks, Dallas," Clint said and he opened his truck's door. The window continued to crackle and fall out of the frame. He reached inside and tried to clear all the glass particles that had fallen on his seat.

His brain had suddenly gone completely numb. The numbness remained with him as he pulled away from the curb and the night air blew in through the open window.

When he was about halfway home, his brain kicked in once again. What the hell had just happened? And more importantly why had it happened?

Was it possible the dead birds and the gunfire were all some sort of a master plan to scare him out of Millsville? For what? What would be the ultimate payoff for somebody? Was this about him seeing Lizzy? Did somebody not like him being with his neighbor?

He didn't want to leave his ranch, but he would in a minute if he thought his daughter was in danger. God, he wished he knew how real the threat was... Was it only a scare tactic or did somebody in his new town really want him dead?

Saturday morning Clint called and asked Lizzy if she wanted to come to his house for coffee. She immediately agreed. She'd hated to turn down his offer of taking her to the Farmer's Club the night before, but she'd needed to meet with Jerry and his men to finish up the harvesting details.

She was eager to see him again. It had been a long week, with the harvesting of her corn, and she'd fallen into bed each night too tired to really even enjoy their nightly phone calls.

Twenty minutes after he called her, she left her house to head over to his. The day was overcast and gloomy and with a threat of rain.

She'd thought a lot about the dead birds in his barn.

The doubt she'd felt about him was gone as common sense took over. Surely if there was something...anything in Clint's past that might be the answer and explain all this, he would have told Dallas. There was no reason why he wouldn't and she was certain Clint wanted it cleared up.

She pulled up and parked, and as always, her heart did a little dance in her chest as she anticipated seeing him again. She knocked and the door was opened. She was hit square in the center by Emily, who hugged her tightly around the waist. "Oh, Ms. Lizzy, I've missed you so much."

"For goodness' sake, Emily, let the poor women get inside the door," Clint said with a laugh.

Emily grabbed Lizzy's hand and pulled her across the threshold and into the house. "Come on in, the coffee is waiting for us," Clint said. He looked as handsome as ever in a pair of worn jeans and a turquoise T-shirt that did amazing things to his eyes.

"Can I have coffee with you?" Emily asked as they walked through the living room toward the kitchen.

"Coffee is just for grown-ups," Clint replied.

"But I'm six years old now, Daddy," Emily said. "I'm not five anymore."

Clint laughed. "I'm sorry, bug, but six doesn't make you a grown-up. You need to go to your room and play with Fifi while we have coffee and grown-up time."

"Ms. Lizzy, will you come and play with me sometime soon?" Emily asked as Lizzy sat in a chair at the table. "We can play mommy doll and baby doll again."

"I'd like that, Emily. We'll make plans to do that again real soon," Lizzy replied.

"'Kay," Emily said, obviously mollified by Lizzy's words.

Minutes later Emily was gone to her bedroom and Clint joined Lizzy at the table, their coffees before them.

"How are you?" he asked. "I feel like we've scarcely talked this last week."

"I know, but thankfully my harvest is done until next year," she said.

"Jerry is going to start mine on Tuesday. I was at the Farmer's Club last night and Walt told me to keep the coffee coming for the men who are working."

"That's sound advice. So, did you have a good time without me?" she asked lightly.

"Of course not. I wouldn't dare have a good time without you," he returned teasingly. "I sat at the bar and visited with Walt. I only stayed for one drink and then I left and I got shot at."

She stared at him blankly, her mind trying to compute what he'd just said. "Excuse me?"

"Somebody shot at me last night as I was getting ready to get into my truck. Thankfully the bullet missed me and instead shot out my driver-side window."

"Oh my gosh, Clint. What the hell?" she asked incredulously. She wrapped her fingers around her cup, seeking its warmth to absorb some of the icy chill that now raced through her. She stared at him. "What on earth is going on, Clint?"

"I wish I knew," he replied grimly. "It's obvious somebody has it out for me, but hell if I know who or why. Most of my interactions here have been with you at my side. Can you think of anyone I might have offended or angered?"

"No…nobody. Does Dallas know about this?"

Clint nodded. "He came to the scene after somebody called him from the bar about an active shooter. Of course, by the time he got there, the shooter was long gone. However, he did manage to dig a bullet out of interior of my truck."

"Good. With the bullet, he'll be able to know what kind of gun was used, then he can check the licenses in the area to find out who all possesses that type of gun."

She gazed at him worriedly. "Oh Clint, who is this person and why is he going after you?"

"God, I wish I knew." He leaned forward, picked up his cup and took a sip. "Has anyone asked you out recently? Has anyone shown an interest in you? Somebody who would want me out of the way?"

"No, Clint. There's nobody like that," she replied firmly. "At this point I wish there was so we'd have an answer for what's going on."

"Dallas had another possible theory," he continued as he returned his cup to the table.

"And what's that?" she asked.

"He wondered if perhaps somebody is just trying to scare me out of town. First with the blackbirds and then by firing a shot at me. My back was a pretty big target for the shooter to miss. Maybe he missed me on purpose. Maybe he doesn't want to kill me at all, but instead, just wants me to leave town."

Lizzy turned over all the information in her mind. She took a drink of her coffee as her brain continued to whirl. "I suppose that could be possible. There's only one real reason why somebody might want to scare you enough that you get out of town."

"And what would that be?" he asked curiously.

"Your land," she replied. "This property and all your fields would be considered highly attractive, prime real estate around here. You've not only got the cornfield but also the wheat fields and pastures as well."

"The wheat wasn't planted last year."

"That doesn't matter, the field is still there. Has anybody approached you about selling this place?"

"No, nobody."

"You bought this ranch without it even being officially on the market for sale. Maybe somebody really wanted this property and they are angry because you beat them to it."

He leaned back in his chair and released a deep sigh. "Or, maybe somebody just wants me dead."

"But why? Clint, I know how you interact with people and I can't believe that you've offended anyone to the point that they would want to kill you. There's got to be something else going on here. Are you sure there's nothing in your past that might be driving this?" She gazed at him intently.

"No...there's nothing in my past that could be causing this," he said after a moment of hesitation. Still, he said it firmly and with a touch of irritation. He swiped a hand through his hair and gazed at her for a long moment.

"I think we should stop seeing each other until this is all sorted out," he said.

She looked at him in stunned surprise. "Oh no, Clint... I don't want that," she immediately protested. "That's the very last thing I want."

"And I don't want you to somehow become collateral damage in this whole mess." He reached across the table and took her hand in his, his gaze now soft and sweet. "God, Lizzy, I wouldn't be able to forgive myself if anything happened to you. The only way to make sure you're safe is to make sure you aren't around me."

"And I want you to be safe," she countered. "But I'm not afraid of being around you. Clint, please don't stop seeing me." She squeezed his hand. "Please don't let this creep ruin things between us." She let go of his hand and once again wrapped her fingers around her coffee cup. "What we've been building is so important to me."

For several long moments they remained silent. She took another drink of her coffee and waited for him to say something.

"I'm going to be busy for the next week or so with the harvesting, so I probably won't be seeing you anyway," he finally said. "We'll see what happens after that."

"Just don't kick me out of your life, at least not over this. If you want to kick me out of your life because you don't care that much about me, then that's another thing altogether," she replied.

"Oh, Lizzy, I definitely don't want to stop seeing you, but I want and need for you to be safe," he replied.

"We can always spend time together here or at my house. We don't have to go out in public to see each other and that should solve the danger issue. Surely we'd be okay to do that."

He smiled at her. "You are one tenacious woman."

She returned his smile. "Only when it comes to people I care about."

"Well, I just wanted to catch you up on what had happened." He paused for a moment and then continued, "Actually, I have one big question to ask you." His eyes darkened and he reached for one of her hands once again.

He enveloped her hand and gazed at her intently. His eyes appeared to be probing deep inside her. "Lizzy, I am all that Emily has in this whole wide world. She has no relatives except for me. What I want to ask you is, if anything bad happens to me, would you take Emily in and raise her?"

She jerked her hand away from his, horrified by his question. "I won't answer that because nothing bad is going to happen to you," she said firmly.

At that moment Emily came dancing into the kitchen with Fifi and the leash in her arms. "Daddy, Fifi just woke up and you told me when she wakes up, then I should take her outside."

"Good girl," Clint said and started to stand.

"Sit tight," Lizzy said. "I'll go outside with her."

"Yeah, I want Ms. Lizzy to go outside with me."

Clint raised his hands in surrender. "Far be it for me to argue with two females."

It took a few minutes to get Fifi on the leash and for the two of them to go outside. Lizzy was aware of Clint standing just inside the door to watch the two of them.

Lizzy's brain still spun in an effort to make sense of the fact that somebody had taken a shot at Clint. She looked around the area, making sure that there was nobody around that might harm her or Emily.

For the first time in her life, she'd found her Mr. Perfect. He was everything she wanted in a man. And now somebody potentially wanted him dead.

He sat in a dilapidated old chair in the living room in the abandoned house he'd been staying in since he'd arrived in the little town. Everything was going as planned.

He was so excited with what he'd already accomplished.

The birds had been easy to get. He'd placed a pan of poisoned corn in the overgrown backyard, and within three days, he'd had seven dead birds, five of them blackbirds. Putting them in a circle in Clint's barn had been genius. He'd wanted to scare the man and he was certain he'd achieved that goal.

He also hadn't wanted to kill Clint with a bullet in the man's back. That was a demise for too easy for the snitch that had put him in prison, for the man who had blabbed to the cops to take away his freedom. He'd only wanted to scare him. He wanted that bullet to stir utter terror in Clint's very heart.

Now he was tired of the easy games and he was ready to move on to the main event. The fear that Clint might have felt with the birds and the bullet was nothing compared to what he was going to feel in the very near future.

He glanced into the kitchen where two wooden chairs sat side-by-side and rope lengths lay on the floor next to them. Excitement roared through him, making him feel half giddy.

Yes, he was ready now to move things along. Now all he had to do was watch and wait for the perfect opportunity to get Emily and Lizzy into those chairs.

A chill of delight raced up his spine as he anticipated how Clint would feel when he saw the two women he loved tortured and then killed. Clint would have those horrific visions in his head right before he died.

Chapter 10

Tuesday morning Lizzy stood at her kitchen window and watched Jerry's combine work through Clint's cornfield. Bailey should be arriving anytime to have lunch with Lizzy, and she was looking forward to catching up with her friend. The two hadn't talked in the last week.

Lizzy had prepared a hot chicken dish and she was also serving a Jell-O salad and homemade biscuits. She turned away from the window and plopped down in one of the chairs at the table to wait for Bailey to arrive.

Clint had been so heavy on her mind, on her heart since she'd left his house on Saturday. She'd tried desperately to think of anyone who might have a grudge against him, but she couldn't come up with anybody.

She now wanted to believe that it was possible it had to do with somebody wanting his farm. The facts that the property had never been on the market officially for sale and Clint had bought it through some kind of connections might have really angered a potential buyer who had just been waiting on a For Sale sign to show up.

Still, no matter how she twisted things around in her mind, she could gain no real clarity about the things that had happened to him. What was all this really about? Who was behind the attack? Who was behind those birds and the gunshot that had come so close to him? Before she could get too far into her dark thoughts once again, her doorbell rang. She jumped up to go greet her friend.

"Hey, girl. What's shaking?" Bailey asked as she followed Lizzy into the kitchen.

As usual, Bailey was dressed stylishly. The blue blouse she wore brought out the blue in her eyes and the navy skinny jeans showcased her long, slender legs. Big blue earrings hung from her ears and a thick blue-and-gold necklace completed her outfit.

"A lot. Have a seat and I'll get lunch on the table," Lizzy said. She pulled the chicken out of the oven and placed the baking dish on hot pads that were in the center of the table. She then got the Jell-O salad out of the refrigerator and added that and the homemade biscuits to the spread.

She finally sat across from her friend. "Dig in and I'll fill you in on things, starting with the fact that Friday night Clint was shot at."

Baily's eyes widened. "'Shot at' like…like…with a gun?"

"Yes, with a gun," Lizzy replied and proceeded to tell Bailey everything that had happened.

"Oh my gosh, what does Dallas have to say about all this?" Bailey asked as she scooped a portion of the chicken casserole onto her plate.

"He has no clue. Clint has no clue and I have no clue," Lizzy replied dispiritedly. "Oh, Bailey, I finally found the man of my dreams, the man I'd like to spend the rest of my life with, and now somebody potentially wants to kill him. What kind of trick is fate playing on us?"

"Hopefully Dallas will be able to arrest the bad guy before anything else happens," Bailey said sympathetically.

"Let's hope so," Lizzy replied.

Bailey grabbed a biscuit and slathered it with butter. "So, if you'd had to answer the question about Emily, what would your answer have been?"

"I'd take her in a minute," Lizzy replied without hesitation. "The last thing I'd want to see for her is to get caught up in the foster care system. I love that little girl and I would never, ever want that for her."

"Wow, you really are in love with Clint and his daughter," Bailey replied.

"I am madly, crazy in love with Clint." It felt good

to finally say the words out loud. "And I love and adore Emily."

"Does he know how you feel about him?" Bailey asked.

"Not exactly. I mean, I haven't told him I'm in love with him yet, but he's got to know how deeply I care for him." Lizzy grabbed a biscuit from the platter. "I slept with him."

"You did? Well, you go, girl," Bailey said in delight. "And how was it?"

"It was wonderfully good," Lizzy replied. Her body warmed with the memories of that night. "He was wonderfully good."

Bailey grinned at her. "Good for you. There's nothing worse than liking a man and then finding out he's awful in bed. If you remember, that's what happened between me and Blane Cookwell. I really liked him until I slept with him. He was such a dud in the bedroom. So, what happens next with you and Clint?"

Lizzy released a deep sigh. "I'm not sure. He wants some distance between us now, until any danger is over."

"As your best friend, that sounds really good to me."

"Well, it doesn't sound good to me," Lizzy replied in frustration. "I don't want any distance between us."

"Lizzy, you have to think about your own safety in all this. You don't want to find yourself in any cross fire that might occur," Bailey said sternly.

"I know. I'm just hoping Dallas can crack this case

wide open in the next day or two, and everyone can breathe easier."

"It's funny, it was only days ago that we were both worried about the Scarecrow Killer, and now you've got something altogether different to worry about."

"Trust me, I'm still scared about our hometown serial killer, but right now, all my focus is on Clint and whoever is after him. Dallas even wondered if this was the Scarecrow Killer playing a new game."

"Well, that's a horrifying thing to think about," Bailey replied.

For a few minutes they ate in silence, the only sound the clinks and scrapes of silverware against their plates. "I taste the crunch of the celery that's in this chicken dish, but there's another crunch. What is that?" Bailey asked.

"Water chestnuts," Lizzy replied.

"You really are a good cook, my friend," Bailey said.

"Since my mother passed away when I was so young and my father was not really into cooking, I had to learn to cook and I've done a lot of experimentation along the way."

Bailey grinned at her. "You're going to make Clint a fabulous wifey."

"Yeah, as long as he stays alive and loves me as desperately and madly as I do him."

"If anyone deserves love and happiness, it's you, Lizzy," Bailey replied. "You give so much of yourself to so many others. It's time you get something wonderful for yourself."

"Thanks, Bailey. Speaking of… What's going on in your love life?"

Bailey snorted. "What love life?"

"You still haven't made a move on Officer Handsome?"

"Not yet, but the good news is I heard through the grapevine that he's not seeing Celeste Winthrop anymore."

"Then, it's the perfect time for you to make your move on him," Lizzy said. "Come on, girl, you've been wanting to date him forever, but you've got to let him know you're available and would like to spend some time with him."

"I know." She released a heavy sigh and then grinned…the naughty grin Lizzy knew so well.

"What?" Lizzy asked.

"I just thought of the perfect way of getting his attention."

"And what's that?" Lizzy already knew it would be preposterous, considering the grin that preceded her idea.

"I can stage a crime in the nail shop…maybe a big theft, and he could come to investigate it and he'll fall madly in love with the poor victim." Bailey smiled with satisfaction.

"Nice fantasy," Lizzy replied with a small laugh. "Only in reality, Dallas or one of the other officers will show up to investigate it. They'll immediately believe it's an inside job and they'll arrest you, put you in jail and then throw away the key."

"Way to be a buzzkill," Bailey replied wryly.

Lizzy laughed. "I'm just trying to keep you on the straight and narrow."

"Yeah, but there's no fun in that. I swear it feels like years since I had my last date." Bailey stood and carried her now-empty plate to the sink.

"It has been a while since you've gone out with anyone," Lizzy replied as the two continued to clear the table.

"Howard Kendall asked me out last week, but I declined his invitation to go to Murphy's with him. I didn't feel like going to the bar, and I figured if he was really interested in me, then he would at least invite me to the café for a meal."

"Did you tell him that?" Lizzy asked.

"No, I didn't want to go out with him that badly anyway."

"Bailey, don't let your mad crush on Officer Benjamin make you not go on dates with other men. Your true love might be the man you turn away, and there's no guarantee that you and Benjamin will really hit it off on a personal level."

"Listen to you, Ms. Happily In Love, telling me what to do in my dating life."

"Oh, Bailey, I just want you to be as happy as I am."

Bailey sighed. "I know." By that time the table was cleared. "I hate to eat and run, but I've got to get back to the shop."

Lizzy walked with her to the front door. "You're always welcome to eat and run here."

"Thanks, I'll call you later and thanks for the great lunch." With that, Bailey left the house.

Lizzy immediately locked the door after her and then headed into the kitchen to put the last of the leftovers away. Once that was done, she went outside and down to where her two ranch hands were unloading a truck full of hay bales and then stacking them in the barn.

"Hey, Jimbo," she greeted the man who had sold her the hay. "My guys treating you all right?"

"Right as rain," Jimbo replied. The hugely overweight man leaned against his truck, a piece of hay poking out of his mouth where two teeth should be. Rumor had it he'd lost his teeth in a bar fight years ago.

Lizzy stepped into her barn where Rory and Tristen were busy stacking what had been unloaded so far. The two men couldn't be more different. Where Rory was a big, fit man with bulging arm muscles and huge thighs. Tristen was a smaller man, with wiry, rather than bulging, muscles.

Where Rory was clean-shaven, Tristen had a short, full dark beard. She wasn't sure what had made her take a chance on Tristen but she was glad that she had. He was a hard worker who with Rory made a good team for her. "How's it going, guys?" she asked.

"It's going," Rory replied as he went back to the truck and hefted another bale of hay up on his shoulders.

"I'll have cold drinks and some sandwiches for you guys up at the house when you all are done here," she said. Normally, she didn't provide any food for her help, but they were doing a big job today with the unloading and stacking of the hay, so she decided they needed some extra attention today.

"That sounds good," Tristen replied.

"That sounds great," Rory added.

"I'll see you both later up at the house," she said, and then with a nod at Jimbo, she turned around and headed back inside. Once there, she paced the floors, often finding herself at the window that looked over to Clint's place.

She could see him standing near the cornfield, watching as the combine did its work. She also recognized all the men who were working there.

Her gaze swept toward the barn and then to the house. She realized she was looking for anyone who might be lurking nearby, anyone who might threaten Clint's well-being. She was on duty, watching over the man she loved as best she could.

If she saw anyone suspicious, she would be over there in a second with her gun drawn. She'd do everything she could to keep the man she loved alive.

Clint collapsed in his chair, exhausted yet satisfied by the day of activity on the ranch. He had one more field that Jerry and his men would get to tomorrow, and then harvest time would be over for him.

Thankfully the price of corn had risen over the

last month or so, so Clint would see more profit in his coffer than he'd initially expected.

He'd gotten Emily in bed and Fifi in her crate for the night, and the house was now silent around him. He wished Lizzy was here. He wished they were sharing one of their deep conversations or their frequent laughter. He missed her when she wasn't with him, and when she was with him, he dreaded the time they would part.

He was in love with her. The realization struck like a thunderbolt out of the clouds. He was completely and totally in love with Lizzy Maxwell, and it wasn't just about his physical attraction toward her.

Somehow she'd sneaked beneath his defenses, she'd managed to fill in the pieces of his heart that had been left aching and empty as he had healed from his wife's death. He would always grieve for Samantha. She'd been his wife for over three years and had been the mother of his precious child.

However, Samantha was gone and would never be returning, and Lizzy was wonderfully alive with her infectious laughter and bright smiles. She was warm and loving and uniquely special. The fact that she loved his daughter so much made her even more amazing and special.

Yes, he'd fought his feelings for Lizzy, but he could fight them no longer. He was deeply in love with her. He wanted to jump in his car and drive over to her house right now to proclaim his love for her, but of course he couldn't do that.

Besides, she deserved far more than a late-night drive-by from him. He'd plan a special evening for her. He'd see if Rosa could take Emily out for a couple hours, maybe on Friday night. Perhaps the two of them could get ice cream or do a little shopping.

He'd buy Lizzy roses. He frowned. No, she didn't really feel like a rose kind of woman. He'd buy her sunflowers. Yes, that felt right. She felt like a sunflower kind of woman.

He'd have champagne and chocolate for their little celebration of love. A tingling excitement rushed through him, along with a delicious heat as he thought about what was to come. This felt good. It felt right in the depths of his very soul. It was time he tell Lizzy exactly how he felt about her and hopefully claim her as his own.

With the warm rush of blood flowing through his veins, he picked up his phone and hit Lizzy's number. She answered on the second ring.

"Are you already in bed?" he asked.

"I just slid in beneath my sheets," she replied.

"I wish I was there with you," he said softly.

"There you go again, Mr. Kincaid, flirting with me and making my head spin," she replied with a small laugh. "And I wish you were here with me, too," she added.

Her words warmed his heart. "I was wondering if you'd like to come over here Friday evening and spend some time with me."

"You know I would love that," she replied. "Just tell me when and I'll be there."

"Why don't we say around seven and if things go right, I'll make you pancakes for breakfast."

She laughed again. "Actually, I've really been in the mood for some pancakes."

They spoke for a few minutes longer and then said their good-nights. He decided to head to bed, even though it was earlier than usual for him. It had been a long day and he suspected tomorrow would be just as wearing.

At least the weather was cooperating. A cold front had moved in, leaving temperatures in the upper sixties during the day. It was a pleasant change from the hot days of summer they'd suffered previously.

He got into bed, closed his eyes and immediately knew no more.

Blood. It was everywhere…spattered on the walls and saturating the curtains at the open window. A baby cried from someplace in the distance. The blood… How was there so much blood? And what was happening on the bed?

Who…who was stabbing his wife? Over and over again, the knife plunged into her, each time spattering more blood on the walls. And still the baby cried and screamed. He stood there momentarily inert as shock overtook him.

"Samantha," he finally yelled her name.

He came awake with a deep gasp. He jerked upright with fight-or-flight adrenaline rushing through him. His heartbeat crashed a frantic rhythm, as feverishly, he gazed around the room.

With the aid of the moonlight shining in the window, his surroundings came into view. He was here in Millsville. He wasn't in the town house in New York City.

It had been far too late for Samantha. The coroner hadn't even been able to count the number of stab wounds she'd received in her stomach. Clint hadn't been able to save her. While his wife was being raped and murdered, Clint had been having a nightcap with some of his coworkers at a local pub. It had taken him a very long time to get over feeling guilty about that drink.

He now scrubbed his hands down his face, waiting for his heartbeat to slow to a more normal rhythm. Geez, he hadn't had that particular nightmare in a long time. Why had he had it now?

Was it because he'd fully embraced his love for Lizzy? Was his past trying to take him back to that place of guilt and grief?

There was nothing for him in his past. He was ready to move on with his life. He refused to feel guilty about finding a new love and building a life with her.

But she doesn't even know your real name, a little voice whispered in the back of his head. *You will never be able to share parts of your past with her.*

Could he be with Lizzy and not tell her the truth about what had happened on the night his wife died?

He believed he could. And there was really no reason why Lizzy had to know about that part of his past. He could share his childhood with her and his teenage years. She knew he'd been married before and that was really all she needed to know.

He settled back in the bed and stared up at the ceiling. Dallas had called earlier in the evening to tell Clint that the bullet that had hit his truck had come from a 9mm gun. Dallas intended to check all the permits and compile a list of people who owned that particular kind of gun, and then he'd get back together with Clint and they'd go over the list.

Clint would love to get the mystery of the dead birds and the shot solved and behind him. He wanted to know who was responsible and why. With questions still swirling around in his head, he finally managed to fall back asleep.

When he next opened his eyes, daylight was just beginning to peek into the window. He got up, took a quick shower and then dressed for the day.

After sitting at the table and drinking two cups of coffee, he went in to awaken Emily so she could get ready for school. They took Fifi outside and then she got dressed for the day. Once she was finished, Clint made her a breakfast of eggs and toast. Not soon after that, Rosa showed up to take Emily to the bus stop.

He asked her about taking Emily out for a couple of hours on Friday night, and to his relief, she agreed to do that. Within a half an hour, Rosa and Emily were gone and Clint headed back to his bedroom.

With his nightmare so fresh in his mind, he felt the need to look through the folder that held newspaper clippings about that particular time in his life.

This time, he was pleasantly surprised to realize they didn't hold as much power as they used to over him anymore. It was like looking at something horrible that had happened in another life…in another time.

He thumbed through them one clipping at a time, reading about the creep who had murdered his wife. He was about halfway through them when a knock fell on his back door. He closed the file and tossed it on the countertop near the coffeepot.

He then opened the door and greeted his ranch hand Reggie. "Hey, boss," Reggie said. "I was just wondering if you want me to keep getting that moldy hay out of the barn today."

"Definitely," Clint replied. "I'd like it done as soon as possible so I can start ordering new hay for the winter." Even though it was only mid-October, the long-term weather report was of an earlier winter than usual.

Thankfully, Reggie had told him the hay in the barn was all bad before Clint had used it to feed his horse and the small herd of cattle he owned. Clint wouldn't have known it was, but it definitely smelled like mildew and mold. He'd thought that might be normal until Reggie had told him it wasn't. Clint had no idea how long the hay had been in the barn.

"Even if I have to work late tonight, I'll get it all done," Reggie replied.

"Thanks, Reggie. And keep track of your extra hours. I'll be glad to pay you overtime."

"That's not necessary," Reggie replied. "Then, I'll just head out to the barn now."

"I'll go with you," Clint said. He locked and closed the door after him. Since Friday night, every time he stepped outside, he half expected a bullet to come whizzing toward him.

They were almost to the barn when Jerry came rumbling up on his combine. A pickup truck with his two men followed. Work on the ranch was officially about to get underway.

It was just after five o'clock when Clint finally made his way back to the house. The corn harvest was done and Reggie was almost finished moving the bad hay to a pasture where they'd eventually do a controlled burn to get rid of it. True to his words, Reggie was working late this evening to get it all finished today.

Clint walked in through the back door. "Daddy!" Emily greeted him. She sat at the table, coloring a picture, but was obviously ready for dinner.

"Hey, bug, how was school today?" Clint leaned over and kissed his daughter's forehead and then smiled at Rosa who was in the process of pulling something that smelled delicious out of the oven. Whatever it was, she slid the large pan onto the stovetop.

"It was good. I got lots of smiling faces on my papers," Emily said.

"That's what I like to hear. I'm very proud of you," he replied. He walked over to the sink and washed up. "How are you doing, Rosa?"

"Can't complain about anything," she replied. "I've heard you aren't doing so well."

Clint glanced as his daughter, who thankfully was concentrating on coloring a picture. "There's been some issues. Rosa, if you aren't comfortable helping me out right now, I'd certainly understand that."

Rosa cast him a warm smile. "Mr. Kincaid, I've lived a nice, long life and when it's my time to go, it's my time to go. I believe I'll be helping you take care of your precious girl until she's so old you won't need me anymore."

He gazed at the older woman warmly. "Rosa, you've been a true treasure to our lives."

"We love you, Ms. Rosa," Emily said.

Rosa's cheeks filled with color. "The meal is ready to eat whenever you are."

"I'm ready now," he replied and took his seat at the table. "I've worked up a real appetite today."

"Me, too, Daddy," Emily said with a smile at him. "A real appetite."

"You've got lasagna and there's salad and garlic bread," Rosa said as she placed the large pan in the center of the table. She got everything on the table. "Now, if you're all set, then I'll just be on my way."

"Thank you, Rosa. We'll see you tomorrow morning," Clint said.

"Bye, Ms. Rosa," Emily added.

While they ate, Emily filled him in on her day. A little boy named Jeffrey refused to sit at his desk when the teacher told him to and so he had to go to time-out. As Emily told him about it, it was obvious she'd been scandalized by the whole thing. "I don't ever want to be in time-out," she concluded. "Time-out is the naughty chair in the corner."

"As long as you keep being a good girl, you won't ever have to be in the time-out chair," he replied.

She then told him that Michelle was her new best friend. Clint didn't know who Michelle was, but Emily adored her and they played together during every recess.

They finished eating and Clint was in the process of finishing the kitchen cleanup when a knock fell on his back door. It was Reggie. He looked as pale as a ghost and he had a bloody towel wrapped around one arm.

"Reggie, for God's sake, what happened?" Clint opened the door wider so Reggie could step inside.

"I was scooping up some of that old hay and there was a broken scythe blade hidden there. Man, it sliced my arm up good."

Clint led him to the sink. "Let's take a look at it."

He unwound the towel and stifled a gasp as he saw the wound. It was a deep, bloody gash. Reggie swayed and then dry heaved. "Sorry, I'm not so good when it comes to blood…especially my own," he said in a faint voice.

Clint wrapped the towel around the wound once again and then led Reggie to a kitchen chair. "You're going to need some stitches. Give me a minute and I'll drive you to the emergency room."

Clint grabbed his phone and called Lizzy. When she answered, he asked if she could come over and watch Emily while he took Reggie to the ER. She immediately agreed and Clint put his phone back into his pocket.

"Hang in there, Reggie. As soon as Lizzy gets here to watch my daughter, we'll take off. Just keep pressure on the cut with the towel," Clint said.

"I'm so sorry to put you out," Reggie said and then moaned.

"Hey, man, I'm sorry you got hurt," Clint replied. "I'll be right back." He headed for Emily's bedroom where she and Fifi were playing. "Ms. Lizzy is going to come over to stay with you for a little while," he said. "Daddy has to leave to run to the hospital."

She looked at him with worry. "Are you sick, Daddy?"

"No, honey, I'm not, but Mr. Reggie hurt himself so I'm going to take him to the hospital to get fixed up."

"Tell Mr. Reggie I hope he gets better," she replied and then giggled as Fifi jumped up to lick her chin.

"I will, and Ms. Lizzy will be here soon."

"I'm so happy about that," Emily said. "We can play baby dolls again."

Clint left her in the bedroom and instead went to the living room to await Lizzy's arrival. Within minutes he saw her truck coming from her place. He went and got Reggie, who still looked too pale and was slightly unsteady on his feet, and led him toward the front door.

Once Lizzy was inside the house, Clint and Reggie were on their way to the hospital. "You doing okay?" Clint asked him.

"As long as I don't see the blood, I'm fine," Reggie replied.

When they arrived at the small hospital, the little ER waiting room was full of people standing around or seated in the green plastic chairs.

Reggie and Clint approached the desk to sign in, and at that time, they learned there had been a three-car pileup on the nearby highway and it might be a while for Reggie to be seen. Clint knew Lizzy would stay with Emily as long as needed, but he pulled his phone out of his pocket and stepped outside to give her a quick call.

"Hey, I'm sorry to say that you might have a longer night there than I intended," he said when she answered. He explained about the car accident. "The ER is completely packed right now and I don't know how long it will be before they get to Reggie."

"It's no problem," she replied. "What time is Emily's bedtime?"

He told her about the bath-and-bedtime routine. "Don't worry, I'll take care of things here," she assured him. "I'll tuck Emily into bed, and then if it gets too late, I might just snooze on your sofa."

"Feel free to make yourself comfortable and at home. There's a blanket in the hall closet if you need it. I'll call you with an update when I can," he replied.

"Don't worry about me. I'll be here," she replied.

He ended the call, warmed by the fact he trusted Lizzy completely with his precious daughter. He suddenly realized darkness had begun to fall and he stood before a brightly lit building, making a perfect target if somebody wanted to take a shot at him. He hurried back inside and sank down in the empty chair next to Reggie.

At least in here with other people milling around, he felt relatively safe. But he definitely couldn't forget that somebody was out to get him, and until that person was caught, he had no idea what to expect next.

Chapter 11

Lizzy sat on the edge of Emily's bed. The little girl smelled of strawberries and the sweet scent of innocence. She brushed a strand of Emily's shiny, slightly damp blond hair away from her face.

Emily had taken her bath and Lizzy had made her laugh, pretending that there were nasty potatoes growing behind her ears. Each time Lizzy spent time with Emily, she found her more and more loving and adorable.

"I like that you're tucking me in tonight," Emily said.

"I like it, too, but I've never tucked in a little girl before. Maybe you can tell me how it's done."

"Well, Daddy and I always take turns telling each

other stories. Would you like for me to tell you a story?" Emily asked.

"Sure, I would like that," Lizzy replied, relieved that she wasn't the one who had to do the storytelling.

Emily told her a story about a cute little dog named Fifi, who went out to explore the farm. She danced in the hay in the barn and then chased a rabbit all around. She went fishing in the pond and caught a huge fish and then spun in circles chasing her tail. Finally Fifi came back into the house, went right into her crate and fell sound asleep, which is what the puppy was doing at this very moment.

"That was a very nice story, Emily," Lizzy said.

"Thank you," Emily replied and then yawned sleepily. "I like to tell stories and I love you so much, Ms. Lizzy," she added.

"I love you, too, sweetie." Lizzy leaned down and placed a gentle kiss on Emily's forehead. "And now go to sleep and have sweet, happy dreams."

Emily gave a half nod as her eyes drifted closed. Lizzy remained on the side of the bed for several more minutes, then sure that Emily was soundly sleeping, she finally got up and left the bedroom.

Clint had called a few minutes before to tell her Reggie still hadn't been seen yet and the wound was still bleeding. He apologized at how long it was taking, but once again, she assured him it was fine. She could always curl up on his sofa and sleep until he got back home.

However, it was way too early for her to want to

do that right now. She decided to go into the kitchen and make herself a cup of coffee. She remembered which cabinets she'd seen Clint use for the filters and the can of coffee.

Unfortunately, he didn't have a single-serve machine. She decided to make a full pot. Maybe when Clint got home, he'd want a cup or two to wind down, despite the lateness of the hour.

As she waited for the coffee to drip through, she saw a file folder nearby on the counter. Lizzy didn't consider herself much of a snooper, but she couldn't help herself. She assumed it might hold financial records or something to do with the farm. She was bored and so she decided to just take a peek inside.

She opened it to find a newspaper article about a murder in New York. She was definitely, immediately intrigued. She poured herself a cup of the freshly brewed coffee and then carried the folder to the kitchen table where she sat and continued to read the first article.

The second article was about the same killer, who had garnered the name the Nighttime Creeper. He was suspected to have raped and killed six women by stabbing them to death.

All the clippings in the folder were about the murders and the man law enforcement sought for arrest. She read every article, a frigid chill growing up inside her.

When she was finished reading all of them, she got up on shaking legs and put the file folder back on the countertop where she'd found it. She sank back down at the table and curled her fingers around the warmth of her cup while her mind whirled with questions.

Why did Clint have this file of horror? Nothing in the clippings mentioned his name. Unless… A new horror filled her. Unless…he was the Nighttime Creeper.

If he was, then he probably had kept the news clippings in the folder so he could enjoy revisiting the crimes he had committed. She'd heard that murderers liked to dwell on their crimes. Some might go to the cemetery where the victims were buried and others might linger around the crime scenes or insert themselves in some way in the investigation.

These news clippings would be a way for him to revisit his crimes. To revel in what he had done. Had he moved here in the middle of nowhere to evade arrest? Was it getting too hot for him to remain in New York?

She wanted to throw up at the very thought. Had she made love with a monster? Had she fallen in love with a serial killer?

No, surely not. Her brain battled against the very idea. Clint was a wonderful, loving father. He'd been caring and good toward her. He couldn't be a serial killer…could he?

However, not that long ago she'd watched a documentary about Dennis Rader, the BTK killer. He'd killed at least ten people. He'd also been a good husband, a churchgoing man and the father of two children. He'd also bound, tortured and killed his victims, hence the nickname of BTK.

So it was possible. Clint could love his daughter dearly and yet kill women in a heinous way. Many serial killers took a hiatus between murders. Was Clint out here merely on a break? Would he eventually go back to killing women? Dear Lord, why had he kept these news stories?

Tears filled her eyes. They were tears of fear… of uncertainty and of loss. She didn't know what to think. She needed Clint to explain this to her and not through a phone call from the emergency room.

She needed to talk to him in person. She also didn't want to have the conversation with him alone, here in his house. She'd invite him out somewhere where she could have the conversation among other people.

God, she was so confused. Who, exactly, was Clint Maxwell?

Before she could form another coherent thought, something smashed down on the back of her head. Pain seared through her skull and a million stars danced in her vision, right before she knew nothing more.

"Take a couple of days off," Clint said to Reggie as they finally left the ER. Reggie had required fifteen stitches to close the gash in his arm and the doctor had prescribed some pain meds for him. "However long you need to heal up, take the time."

"I hate this," Reggie replied miserably. "I feel like I'm completely letting you down."

"Reggie, don't be ridiculous. You got hurt." The two men got into Clint's truck.

"Yeah, but I know how badly you wanted that hay out of the barn," Reggie said once they were buckled up.

"It can wait and I can do it myself," Clint replied. He started his engine and pulled out of the hospital parking lot. "Unfortunately, it's too late tonight to get that script filled for you."

"It's okay, I'll fill it sometime tomorrow if I need it. Right now, it isn't hurting too badly."

"That's because the doctor numbed it up to stitch it. Once that numbing medicine wears off, it's probably going to hurt like hell," Clint replied.

"I'll be fine," Reggie replied. "Sorry I got so woozy there for a minute. The sight of blood definitely always gets to me. I've always been that way. My older brother used to make fun of me for it."

"I promise I won't spread it around that you're a complete wuss when it comes the sight of blood," Clint said, making Reggie laugh. "Are you sure you can drive home from my place?" he asked on a more serious note. "I'd be glad to take you so you don't have to drive right now."

"Thanks for the offer, but I'll be fine driving myself home. I'll be just fine," Reggie replied. "But I really appreciate you taking me to the ER. Some bosses wouldn't have been so nice."

"It was no problem." However, Clint was more than ready to get to his own place and call it a night. It was after midnight. He guessed that Lizzy would probably be asleep on the sofa. He hated that he would wake her when he came into the house, but it couldn't be helped.

Maybe she'd go ahead and finish out the night with him. He would love to spoon her warm body with his as they both drifted off to sleep.

The two men chatted a bit more and before long they were back at the farm. Clint pulled up and parked, and then the two of them got out of the truck. "Just call me when you're ready to come back to work," Clint said as he walked with Reggie toward Reggie's truck.

"Will do," Reggie replied. "I should only need a couple of days off. I'd say I'll be back by next Monday."

"Sounds good to me," Clint replied. He waited until Reggie was in his truck, and once he pulled out of the driveway, Clint turned to head inside.

Before he got to his front door, a text sounded on his phone. He paused in his tracks and pulled his phone out of his pocket. He almost never got texts. Even Lizzy rarely texted him.

Peek-a-boo. I see you.

Clint stared at the words. What the hell? What did that mean? And he didn't recognize the phone number the text had come from. He looked around the area but saw nobody.

With a bit of unease, he unlocked his front door and stepped inside. He walked into the living room and was surprised that Lizzy wasn't on the sofa. Maybe she'd decided to crawl into his bed to sleep, he thought.

He walked down the hallway to his bedroom, but Lizzy wasn't there, either. A bit of anxiety swept through him. She had to be here somewhere. Her truck was still outside. He peeked into Emily's room and terror gripped his heart, his very soul. Emily wasn't there. Her bed was empty.

What in the hell was going on? "Lizzy," he yelled. He waited, but there was no response. "Lizzy," he shouted even louder. Where were they? Where could they be? Dear God, what was happening?

His text went off again. He yanked the phone out of his pocket.

Welcome to your nightmare.

Clint stared at the words, for a moment frozen in place, as an icy chill raced up and down his spine. The two females who were closest to his heart were gone, and he knew now they had been taken from the house. He realized now that they were in danger. Fear ripped through him. Who had them and where were they?

Dallas. Clint needed the police here immediately.

He called 9-1-1. As he waited for the police to arrive, he walked through the rooms, looking for something…for anything that might provide a clue.

His blood chilled all over again as he found the point of entry. His bedroom window was broken out. Somebody had come in through his window, and whoever it was had somehow taken Lizzy and Emily. Dear God, where were they now?

Minutes ticked by, dreadful minutes of not knowing anything, of being terrified as to what might be happening to his loved ones. Where was Dallas? Clint wanted to call in the FBI, the US Marshals and the CIA. He wanted everyone in town out searching for Lizzy and Emily.

He stood at the front door, waiting for Dallas to arrive. What was taking him so long? It felt like it was hours ago that Clint had called for help. Finally he saw the swirl of red-and-blue lights coming down the road. Dallas pulled in first, followed by several more patrol cars with officers.

Clint quickly ushered them all inside. "They're gone. Lizzy and Emily have been kidnapped," he blurted out the moment the men were all in the house. "They're gone and I got two weird texts right before I walked into the house. Who took them? Where are they? Dallas, we have to find them as soon as possible. We need to search for them right now. They must be in danger."

"Whoa, Clint, slow down. I know you're frantic,

but let's back up a bit. Where were you when all this happened?"

He quickly explained about having to go to the ER with Reggie and that Lizzy had come over to stay with Emily. "I came home and discovered they were both gone. There's a broken window in my bedroom and that's how he must have gotten inside."

He sighed with frustration. Every minute they were in here talking was another minute nobody was out searching for Emily and Lizzy. He had to find them before something bad happened to them. He absolutely refused to entertain the notion that it was already too late.

"You mentioned some strange text messages," Dallas said.

Clint nodded and pulled them up on his phone so the lawman could read them. "And you don't recognize the number associated with them?"

"No, I don't recognize it at all."

"You have no idea who might have sent them to you?" Dallas asked.

"None," Clint replied. His heart still beat with a frantic beat, and adrenaline flooded his veins. Terror gripped him by the throat, half closing off his air. Where were the two people he loved more than anything else in the world?

Dallas turned to the four officers who had come in with him. "Search the property," he told them. "Look in every nook and cranny in the barn and any of the other outbuildings."

"Got it," one of the men said, and then the four of them headed outside.

"I'm going to check that window," Dallas said and headed toward the bedrooms.

Clint remained in the living room, his heart pounding so hard he felt half-sick. He couldn't imagine his baby girl frightened and crying out for him and him not being there to hold and comfort her.

Was it possible this was about his past? What else could it be? Had he finally been found? Or was this because of the present? Was the person who had done this the same person who had left the dead blackbirds and taken a shot at him? He hated to blow his cover if this wasn't about his past.

However, he would blow his cover in a minute if he thought it could save Lizzy and Emily. His baby girl... What was his sweet, innocent daughter experiencing right now?

That sick feeling rose up inside him again as he thought of Emily in the hands of a madman. Then, there was Lizzy. God, this couldn't happen again. He couldn't lose another woman he loved to murder. God, this could not be happening.

Dallas came back to the living room. "It looks like it was a clean entry. I'll have one of my officers check it for fingerprints, but I didn't see any loose threads from clothing or anything else that might provide a clue."

"And if he was smart enough to pull this off, then

he was probably smart enough to wear gloves," Clint replied miserably.

"I'm calling in some more men so we can do a wider search," Dallas said. "There's not many places in town where a person could hide a woman and a child, but there are some. Hopefully we'll find them before the night is over."

"I want them found right now," Clint replied vehemently. "I swear I don't know why this is happening. I can't imagine who would do such a thing."

"We need to do a complete search of the house, and if you see anything amiss in any of the rooms, you need to let me know," Dallas said.

"I feel like we're just wasting precious time," Clint protested. "We know they aren't here."

"But we don't know everything that happened here. We could find a major clue in any of the rooms. We need to clear the entire house to make sure we don't miss anything that could help us in the search," Dallas replied firmly.

For the next twenty minutes or so, the two men checked each and every room in the house, looking for anything amiss. There was nothing to indicate that the kidnapper had left anything behind or had even been in any of the rooms.

There was no way to tell whether Emily had been in bed when she'd been taken, or maybe she'd had one of her nightmares and Lizzy had comforted her by allowing her to come out to the sofa. Or maybe both of them had been in his bed and the kidnapper had somehow snatched them from there. How had this happened?

How had somebody managed to control both Lizzy and Emily and take them out of the house? The kidnapper had to have had a gun. The gun that was supposed to protect Lizzy was probably still in her purse, and her purse was on the end table in the living room.

There were so many unknowns, and so Dallas deemed the entire house as a crime scene. More officers arrived and Dallas gave them instructions for continuing the search around Clint's property.

They had just come back into the living room when Clint's phone rang with another text.

It's Nighttime where I am. I feel like Creeping about.

Clint stared at the words. His gut tightened and his heart plummeted to the pit of his stomach and beat a new rhythm of terror. Now he knew, his past had definitely caught up with his present.

Dallas read the words and then looked at Clint with a frown. "Does that mean anything to you?" he asked.

"Yeah, it means I need to have a conversation with you right now." It was time Clint came clean about his past because it may be the only way to somehow save Lizzy and Emily.

Clint sank down in his chair and motioned Dallas to the sofa. "It all happened four years ago," he began despite the clock ticking in his head.

"I decided to go out with some buddies for a drink after work. It was about eight-thirty...after dark... when I got back to the town house where I lived with my wife and daughter."

The back of his throat threatened to close up as he went back to that horrible place and time. "I... I walked in the front door and immediately heard a kind of scuffling and grunting sound coming from my bedroom, and Emily was in her crib in her nursery screaming and crying."

Clint swallowed hard against the emotion that rose up inside of him. It was a sick emotion of terrible trauma. It was definitely the stuff of nightmares. "I... I walked into the bedroom and a man was on top of my wife, Samantha, and he was stabbing her over and over again. The blood... Oh God, Dallas, there was so much blood. It was dripping down the walls and the curtains. Anyway, Samantha was dead. The attacker jumped through the open bedroom window and disappeared, but not before I got a very good look at him. The killer had already raped and killed six women, and he was nicknamed the Nighttime Creeper."

Clint drew in a deep breath and then continued, "Two months later the police called me about doing a suspect ID. They showed me a dozen pictures of different men and I immediately identified the killer."

He sat up straighter in his chair. "Dallas, I need to be out there searching for them right now."

"I have men out looking. What you need to do is finish telling me what happened so I have all the tools I need to find them," Dallas said firmly.

"To make a long story short, his name is Wayne Lee Gossage, and he went to trial and received life in prison without the possibility of parole. I was the prosecutor's star witness. At the trial, he made some vile threats not only against me but against my two-year-old daughter as well."

Clint got up from the chair, went into the kitchen and grabbed the file folder he'd kept about the crimes and the man who had murdered his wife. He handed Dallas the papers.

"For the next couple of years I tried to rebuild my life in New York, and then the FBI contacted me because Wayne had escaped prison, and just before he did, he once again threatened me and Emily. So they offered me witness protection and that's what brought me here. My real name is Joe... Joe Masterson...and I think we can assume that Wayne Lee Gossage now has my daughter and Lizzy, and eventually, he'll come for me." Horror mingled with a deep grief inside Clint as he thought of how his wife had died. "Dallas, he's the most depraved, immoral man you'll ever run into. I'm sure now he was the one who put the blackbirds in my barn and took a shot at me."

"How is this guy operating here? Does he have a vehicle? Does he own property here?" Dallas frowned in obvious frustration. "He has to be staying somewhere around here and he has to have a way to get money."

"All I can tell you is that he comes from very wealthy parents who believed in his innocence despite the facts, so he's probably getting money through that channel," Clint replied. "I need to go, Dallas. I need to do something to find them," he added. A sick adrenaline filled him as he once again got out of the chair.

"Clint, the best thing you can do right now is stay here and let my men do the searching. If you want to be helpful then go make a pot of coffee. I have a feeling it's going to be a very long night."

Wayne Lee Gossage sat in his truck parked behind the old, abandoned house. He'd done it. After knocking Lizzy over the head into unconsciousness, he'd sedated her and then he'd crept into Emily's bedroom, where the kid was sound asleep, and he'd sedated her as well.

Aware of time ticking and not knowing exactly how long Joe would be gone from the house, he had quickly carried the little girl out of the room and out of the house to his pickup with the covered bed. He'd placed her there and then hurried back in to carry Lizzy out.

As he'd driven away from Joe's farm, a giddy

excitement had rushed through him. He'd done it. He'd really done it. He'd managed to snatch the two most important females in Joe's life right out from under his nose.

Emily and Lizzy were now tied firmly in the two straight-backed chairs in the kitchen. He suspected they would remain unconscious until sometime in the morning.

Joe would be beside himself. He must have been half-hysterical when he'd found them both missing. Wayne hoped he felt utter, bone-chilling terror. And when he realized Wayne had them and as the night continued with no answers, Wayne hoped Joe felt the very depths of despair.

Wayne grabbed the pillow from the passenger side and then adjusted the driver seat so he could get comfortable for the night. He slept in the truck on the off chance that somebody might find him here. If he sensed anyone around, then he could start the engine and make a quick getaway.

The last thing he wanted to do was to go back to prison. He was so much smarter than the other inmates there. He was so much more intelligent than the guards. He deserved more than a life behind bars. Those women he'd killed had deserved to die. They'd been useless and weak, just like his mother had been.

In the meantime, he had so much fun to look forward to. He had a helpless woman and a child who he would eventually torture and kill, but only if Joe was in the room to see it.

And then he'd kill Joe...the witness who had sent him to prison for life, with no hope of parole.

Chapter 12

The night crept by in agonizing increments of time. Clint's kitchen had been turned into a crime center, with a map of the town on the table and officers coming in and out to report and get new assignments to further the search.

Clint poured cups of coffee for the men and paced the floors. His brain had gone numb, as if it was unable to sustain the horror...the true terror that threatened to consume him completely.

The fact that Wayne Lee Gossage was behind the kidnappings only increased the utter agony that ripped through him. Clint knew how depraved, how utterly soulless Gossage was, and he couldn't believe that the man now had Clint's sweet, beautiful daughter and the woman he loved in his hands. But no matter how hard it was to believe, that was the horrifying truth of the matter.

Minutes turned into hours and still there was no news. Somebody ordered pizza, but the very smell of it made Clint half-nauseated. How could he even think about eating anything when he didn't know where his daughter was? How could he eat when he didn't know where Lizzy was being held?

And with each minute that passed, the hope that the two would be found alive and well began to wane. The officers had not only checked out all his outbuildings by now but Lizzy's as well, and now they were fanned out in different directions seeking where the two females might be being detained.

They had spoken with Gladys, who owned the house on the other side of Lizzy's, to see if she had heard or seen anything that might be helpful, but unfortunately, she had no information to offer them.

There was no near neighbor on the other side of Clint's property. There were several pastures in between the houses, so there was really no reason to believe that particular person would have seen or heard anything at Clint's place. Still, Dallas made sure that neighbor was questioned.

Clint went back to Emily's room and sank down in the rocking chair in the corner of the room. There had been many nights when she'd been younger that he'd rocked her in his arms. He'd hummed the tune of "You Are My Sunshine" until she'd fallen asleep.

Now his arms were achingly empty. But her scent lingered in the room, a smell of strawberries and girlhood and innocence. Tears filled his eyes. He swiped them away, but they continued to fall. Faster and faster, they raced down his cheeks until he was sobbing with emotion. Fear coupled with loss pressed tight against his chest.

He got up and found Ms. Sparkles on the bed. It was a white teddy bear in a pink tutu with glitter interwoven into the nylon. Ms. Sparkles was Emily's favorite stuffed animal and the bear always slept with her.

But tonight, she was out there somewhere in the dark of night, frightened and alone without Ms. Sparkles by her side...without him by her side. This caused a new wave of grief to stab through him, and more tears fell from his eyes. He returned to the rocker with the bear in his arms.

He wasn't sure how long he sat crying, but finally he managed to pull himself together. He drew in several deep, long breaths, fighting the exhaustion that pulled at him.

He couldn't be exhausted... He couldn't rest until Emily was happily back in her bedroom. He couldn't sleep until he knew the two most important people in his life were safe and sound.

He must have been back in the bedroom, crying, for some time, because when he emerged, he was shocked to realize that the morning sun was rising.

The long dark night had gone by with no answers forthcoming, but dawn renewed his hope that today they would be found. It would be far easier to search for them in the light of day.

Was it already too late? He refused to allow those words to linger for too long in his brain. It couldn't be too late for them. He wouldn't be able to live if it was too late.

"Morning," Dallas said. The lawman looked as exhausted as Clint felt.

"I guess there's nothing new," Clint said as he walked to the counter to pour himself a cup of coffee.

"Nothing yet," Dallas replied. "We're widening our search. If he's someplace in Millsville, we'll find them." There was a determined ring in the lawman's voice.

Clint carried his coffee to the table and sat down. "Rosa stopped by earlier this morning and I sent her on home. She said she'd heard the news and she wanted to be here for you," Dallas said.

"That was very kind of her," Clint replied, touched by the older woman's desire to help. Still, he was grateful that Dallas had sent Rosa home. There was really nothing she could do, and the fewer people underfoot, the better.

"Let me show you the areas we've already searched," Dallas said and directed Clint's attention to the map on the table.

"Every place that's marked in red has been searched," he explained.

Even though Clint was depressed by the lack of results, he had to admit he was very impressed by how much ground the search had covered so far. Apparently, the officers had been very busy overnight.

Dallas had instructed one officer to go back to the police station and find a good picture of Wayne Lee Gossage. Once a good photo was found, he then wanted fifty copies made so that anyone involved in the search would have a good visual of who, exactly, they were trying to find.

The copies were now on the table, but Clint found it difficult to look at them. He'd hoped to never see that hateful face again.

He didn't want to look at the man who had killed his wife and destroyed his life once before, the man who had the ability now to destroy him and his life for a second time.

The pizza from the day before was gone, but several boxes of donuts had replaced it. Once again, Clint found himself pacing the floors as Dallas's officers continued to come in and out of the house.

At about nine o'clock a knock fell on the front door. Clint went to answer with Dallas hot on his heels. He opened the door and found about a dozen people standing outside.

Walt stood before the others. "We all heard about Lizzy and your little girl missing and we're here to help with the search," he said.

Clint recognized Harper Brennan from the Sweet Tooth Bakery and Bailey from the nail shop and several of the men he'd met at the Farmer's Club. There were also many people he didn't know by name but that he'd seen around town.

For a moment Clint couldn't speak around the large lump in the back of his throat. These people had come to help, with nobody forcing them, with nobody pushing them. They were here strictly out of good will and it spoke to how much Lizzy was liked in the town. It spoke of a community Clint hadn't realized he belonged to.

"Thank you…thank you all," Clint finally managed to reply. He was embarrassed by the tears that burned at his eyes once again. "I'm sure Lizzy would be very happy to know how you've all turned out for her."

"Hell, Clint, we're not just here for Lizzy. You've become one of us and we've turned out for you, too," Walt said. "Now, tell us how we can help."

"I'll leave that up to Dallas," Clint said with thick emotion once again pressing tight against his chest. He let Dallas step forward to address all the people.

Clint barely listened as Dallas told who to go where. It was a beautiful, cool autumn day, but all he saw was death in the leaves that had turned different colors. Some of them had withered up and drifted down to the ground in a death spiral. He felt as if he was in a death spiral.

He closed his eyes for a long moment. How long did he have to exist in this torturous limbo of not knowing where Lizzy and Emily were, of not knowing if they were dead or alive? He fully expected

Gossage to contact him again, but when? How long would the man make him wait?

Dallas gave the volunteers their orders, and then he and Clint returned to the kitchen. They'd only been there a few minutes when an officer came in and asked to speak to Dallas privately.

Dallas led the officer down the hallway, where the two spoke in hushed whispers Clint couldn't hear. What was going on? Had something happened? The muscles in Clint's stomach clenched tight.

The two came back into the kitchen. "I need to go check something out," Dallas said. He looked as tense as Clint had ever seen him.

"What?" Clint asked, a new apprehension tightening his chest as he stared at Dallas.

"It's nothing," Dallas said, not quite meeting Clint's gaze.

"Dallas, don't play with me. What's going on?" Clint replied.

The lawman released a deep breath. "There's a woman's body at the base of one of the silos. She was found by a couple of farmers."

"Why are you trying to leave me out of the loop?" Clint asked angrily.

"I was merely going to check it out before telling you anything," Dallas replied. "All we know right now is that she's blonde…and she's dead."

Clint stared at Dallas in a new horror. "Is…is it Lizzy?" he finally managed to ask.

"I don't know. Apparently, she's facedown so no

identification has been made yet. I need to take a couple of men and go check it out," Dallas said.

"One of the men you're taking is me," Clint said firmly.

"Clint, it would be best for you if you stay here," Dallas protested.

"To hell with that. If...if it's Lizzy, then I need to be there. I can either ride with you or I'll take my truck. I know where the grain silos are," Clint replied in determination.

Dallas stared at him for a long moment. "Okay, then let's go."

Clint grabbed his phone and then followed Dallas out to his patrol car. His heart beat the rhythm of deep dread as he got into the passenger seat.

"Do you know what clothes Lizzy was wearing when she was kidnapped?" Dallas asked as he started his engine.

"I don't know," Clint replied. "Things were so chaotic with Reggie hurt and needing to go to the hospital, I didn't pay attention."

He should have paid attention. He should know what his lover had been wearing when she'd come to sit with Emily. Oh God, it couldn't be Lizzy, he thought. *Please don't let it be Lizzy.* He could swear he felt his heart physically breaking. And if it was Lizzy, then where was Emily?

A patrol car followed close behind Dallas's vehicle. Clint wanted them all to drive faster. He needed to know if Lizzy was really dead.

The bright sunlight seemed like a personal affront to the grief that pierced through him. It should be a dark and gloomy day when death came to call. *Please don't let it be Lizzy*, his heart cried again.

The silos in the distance drew closer and closer, and with each mile Dallas drove, Clint's stomach and chest tightened with both dread and fear.

"Maybe it was a false report," he said aloud.

"That would be nice, but it's doubtful," Dallas replied. "The two men who found her are credible. You have to prepare yourself, Clint. It's very possible we're about to find Lizzy."

Not again, Clint thought. Dammit, he couldn't stand the thought of losing another woman who he loved. Lizzy had his heart, he'd hoped that she would be his future. And now she was probably dead. He could hardly stand it.

Finally they reached the parking area in front of the silos. Clint jumped out of the car and immediately saw the body at the base of the main one. The woman was clad in a pair of jeans and a blue blouse, exactly like something Lizzy would wear.

She was facedown, her blond hair around her head. As Dallas, the other two officers and Clint approached, Clint felt as if he might throw up.

He wanted them to turn her over as quickly as possible, but Dallas stopped him in his tracks. "There are some things we need to do before we move her," he said. "You just stand tight right here for a little while."

Clint wanted to scream in protest, but he managed

to hold himself together while one of the officers took dozens of photos and the other officer, along with Dallas, checked the area around the body.

Clint stared at the female. Were the legs thinner than Lizzy's or was that just part of his need at work to make this body be somebody else? Was the blond hair as long as Lizzy's? *Don't be her,* his heart cried. *Please don't be Lizzy.* But there was no question that it could be her.

Finally it was time for the moment of truth. Dallas gently rolled the woman over and Clint fell to his knees with a deep sob of relief. It wasn't Lizzy.

She appeared younger than Lizzy and definitely thinner. The cause of death seemed to be a drug overdose, as a needle was still stuck in the poor woman's arm. Dallas made a phone call to Josiah Mills, who was both the undertaker and the coroner, to come out and then he turned to Officer Joel Penn and told him to take care of the scene.

"Call in whatever help you need. I'm heading back to Clint's house," he said.

Dallas then motioned Clint back to his patrol car. For a few minutes they drove in silence. "Her name is Regina Wells," Dallas said, finally breaking the silence between them. "She's been addicted to heroin for a long time. I imagine that's what killed her."

"That's so sad," Clint said.

"It is sad. Lots of people tried to help her along the way, but I guess ultimately her demons won," Dallas replied.

"And speaking of demons, the real question is, once again, where is Lizzy and where is my daughter?"

Lizzy came to slowly, a splitting headache tightening across her forehead. As she attempted to raise her arm to her head, she realized she couldn't. Her arm must be twisted in the sheets. She tried to lift it again, but to no avail.

As more consciousness cleared her head, she slowly opened her eyes and then gasped. What was happening? Oh God, what was going on? She was tied tightly in a chair in what appeared to be an abandoned kitchen.

She opened her mouth to release a scream, but before any sound could escape from her, she turned her head and saw Emily, tied into a chair next to her.

A new horror filled her at the sight of the little girl, who apparently remained unconscious. Lizzy didn't want to wake her. The less time Emily spent in this…this nightmare, the better.

And this was a nightmare. Sweet Jesus, who had done this to them? Why were they here? Despite her nauseating headache, she frowned and thought about the night before. Maybe remembering what had happened last evening would give her an idea of who had brought them here.

There had been an accident and Clint had taken his ranch hand to the hospital. She had tucked Emily into bed and then…and then she'd looked into the file folder.

Clint. Oh God, was he the monster who had brought them here? Had he killed all those women in New York and moved here to escape law enforcement, but his urge…his need to kill had reemerged?

She thought of all the times things hadn't quite made sense with him. The fact that he'd never ridden a horse before… Emily telling her that her name had once been Natalie. Now they all seemed bigger issues than they had been at the time. She now remembered the dark shadows that had jumped into his eyes when anyone asked about his past.

Had Clint put the blackbirds in a circle in his own barn? Had he been the one to shoot out the window in his truck that night at the Farmer's Market? Had he been building a case that somebody was after him so he could kidnap her and Emily? It sounded so preposterous, and yet that file folder made her believe it was possible.

Maybe he saw Millsville as new hunting grounds, and Lizzy and Emily were going to be his first victims in his new town. Still, why would he kill sweet little Emily now?

It just didn't feel right. Despite the things that didn't quite make sense, the man she'd come to know, the man she'd watched father Emily… It didn't feel like there was any part of evil…of monster inside him.

However, she was left with the same question. Who was the real Clint Kincaid? There was no question that she'd occasionally seen dark shadows in his eyes. Still, her heart felt like it knew his and she'd seen only goodness there. But was it possible that he could be a complete psychopath? Or maybe a schizophrenic? She supposed at this point anything was possible.

She worked her hands together in an effort to try to escape the rope that held them. Frantically she pulled and tugged, yanked and twisted, but there was no give.

She finally stopped, gasping with her efforts, and her wrists now burning in agony. She looked around the room to find something…anything she could use to help her get free.

The kitchen cabinets were half broken out and a thick layer of dust covered all the countertops. They were obviously in one of the abandoned homes that dotted the area.

Was anyone out looking for them? Did anyone even know that they were missing? Her ranch hands might realize she wasn't home. But they would probably see her pickup parked at Clint's and would assume she was just fine.

If Clint was behind all this, then nobody would be out looking for them. Nobody would even know they were missing. The questions that whirled around in her brain only intensified her headache.

At that moment Emily came to. She looked around wildly and then focused on Lizzy. "Ms. Lizzy, wha— what is this? Why are we tied up?" She began to cry.

"What is happening? I'm too scared. Ms. Lizzy, I'm so scared."

"Don't cry, honey," Lizzy said, wishing she could draw the frightened little girl into her arms. "It's a game, Emily. It's just a silly game." Lizzy didn't know what else to say to Emily in an attempt to assuage her fear.

"Well, I don't like this game," Emily said amid tears. "I don't want to play this game anymore."

"I don't like it, either, but hopefully somebody will come soon and untie us," Lizzy said and attempted to force a lightness in her voice.

Emily continued to weep, and the sobs of the little girl ripped through Lizzy's heart. Lizzy wanted to weep, too. But she had to keep it together for Emily's sake. Emily cried for a little while longer, and then thankfully, she fell back asleep.

Morning sun drifted through the nearby filthy window and dust motes danced in the air. Lizzy tried once again to get her hands free. She yanked and pulled until a bead of sweat formed on her forehead and her wrists once again screamed in pain.

She had to get free before the person who held them captive returned. She felt the emptiness of the house around them and knew they were all alone, but for how long?

A sob escaped her and she had to stop trying to get her hand free. Her wrists were raw and she wouldn't be surprised if they were bleeding. And still there was no give to the ropes.

Tears chased down her cheeks. She tried to cry as quietly as possible. The longer Emily slept, the better. It was a way for her to escape this…this horror.

She stiffened as she heard footsteps on gravel. Somebody was coming. Clint? If he walked through the door right now, she'd be absolutely devastated. Her heart would be completely destroyed. And yet, who else could it be?

The footsteps came closer and closer, and a door opened and then banged shut. She gasped as the man walked into the kitchen.

"Tristen." She stared at the man who was her ranch hand. "Tristen, for God's sake, what's going on here? Why have you done this to us? Please, let us go. If you let us go right now without anyone getting hurt, I won't tell anything to anyone about this."

Tristen grinned, but it was a smile that chilled her blood. It didn't soften the utter blackness of his eyes. "Now, why would I want to let you go after I went to so much trouble to get you here?"

"Why? Why is this happening?" She looked at him searchingly. "What have we done to you?"

"You're nothing to me. You're simply a means to an end," he replied.

"What end?" Lizzy half yelled with fear and frustration. She swallowed hard in an effort to get her emotions under control. She didn't want to wake up Emily and, in any case, she needed to try to stay calm to try to talk Tristen into letting them go.

"You should ask Joe," he replied.

She frowned. "Who is Joe?" What in the hell was he talking about?

"Ah, I thought Clinty boy might have already told you by now. His name isn't Clint... It's Joe... Joe Masterson. He's a serial killer and he killed my wife. I'm here to make sure he never kills anyone else again."

She continued to stare at him, unsure if she believed in his words or not. She hadn't seen the name Joe Masterson in those newspaper clippings.

"So, what does all this have to do with me and with Emily?"

"You two have to die because Joe loves you," he said with another one of his sick grins. "It's the only way to punish him in the way he needs to be punished."

"Tristen, think of another way to punish him," she replied frantically. "This will just make you a serial killer like him. Besides, killing me won't hurt him... He, uh, broke up with me two nights ago. He told me he didn't care about me anymore. And as far as Emily is concerned, he's really tired of being a parent to her. He asked me if I or somebody else I might know would be interested in adopting her."

She shot a quick glance sideways and wanted to cry as she saw Emily's innocent blue eyes staring at her with a hurt expression. Oh God, she hoped she got the opportunity to tell the child at some point that she was lying and her father loved her very much.

"Why don't you let Emily go? She's just a little

girl. You could let her go and still have me," Lizzy said the words in a frenzied tone. "Just untie her and let her run. I don't know where we are, but I would imagine it will probably take her some time to find any adults and she'll never be able to lead anyone back here. Just let her go, Tristen."

"Nice thought, but it's not going to happen. And now I'm going to head outside to enjoy a little bit of this beautiful weather." He laughed. "It's a beautiful day to die." He walked out the doorway that was in the kitchen and then disappeared from sight.

"He's a bad man," Emily exclaimed.

"You're right, honey. He's a very bad man, but while he's gone, I want you to know that I lied to him about your daddy. Your daddy loves you very, very much and he would never, ever give you away to anyone. But, honey, I might have to lie some more to the bad man, and you shouldn't believe the things I say or get your feelings hurt. Okay?"

"'Kay," she replied. Her lower lip trembled ominously. "I just really, really want to go home, Ms. Lizzy."

"Me, too, honey. Me, too. See if you can get your hands untied." She hoped Emily's ropes were looser than hers. Maybe Emily could actually escape her binds and then she could help Lizzy with hers. "But when the bad man comes back inside, you have to sit in your chair very still."

"While you try to get your hands free, I'll tell

you a story," Lizzy said in hopes of keeping Emily's mind occupied with something other than her fear.

She told the story about a little dog named Fifi who went into town for a visit. She made it as silly as possible and was rewarded with Emily's giggles.

Lizzy knew how important it was that she keep her wits about her, but she had never known such yawning terror in her entire life.

Clint paced the floor in his living room. His eyes felt gritty from lack of sleep, his body ached and his heart hurt more than it ever had.

Officers and townspeople came in and then left again after receiving new instructions from Dallas. Two FBI agents had arrived earlier and were now working with Dallas.

The afternoon sun rose higher in the sky, and for the first time since the two had gone missing, Clint's hope at finding the two alive waned.

Would their bodies be found in shallow graves somewhere? Or would they be found in a barn, half-covered with hay? When these kinds of dreadful thoughts crawled into his head, he tried to shove them away as quickly as possible. However, it was growing more and more difficult not to have those images as the sun continued to brighten and rose higher.

It was early afternoon when Clint's phone rang. He ran into the kitchen and saw that it was an anonymous caller. He answered with a terse hello.

"Are we having fun yet?" a deep voice asked.

Icy chills raced through Clint as he recognized the voice of Wayne Lee Gossage.

"Where are they?" Clint asked. He couldn't help the desperation that deepened his voice.

"Don't worry, they're fine...for now," Wayne replied.

"What do you want, Gossage?"

"I want you to be here with us. I want you here when I torture your lover and daughter. I want you to be here when I finally kill them and then kill you." Gossage growled the words.

"Just let them go, Gossage. They're innocent in all of this. I'm the one you want...just let them go."

Gossage merely laughed, a sound that ripped through Clint's guts.

Dallas scribbled a question on a notepad and showed it to Clint. "How do I know they aren't already dead? I need proof of life," he said after reading the note.

"And I need proof of life from you," Wayne replied.

"What in the hell are you talking about?"

Clint wanted to crawl into the phone and wrap his hands around Wayne's neck. He wanted to squeeze the very life out of the man who had taken Lizzy and Emily, but not before he knew where Emily and Lizzy were.

"I want front page coverage in the newspaper. I'm better than that stupid Scarecrow Killer and I want the whole town to know that," Wayne said with more than a touch of arrogance in his voice.

"I can't arrange that until tomorrow morning. I need proof of life from you right now," Clint replied firmly.

"Hang on." There was several moments of silence.

"Daddy, please come and get me. A bad man has us and I'm… I'm scared." Emily little voice came over the phone and pierced straight through to the very center of Clint. He nearly fell to his knees at the sound of her so frightened and him unable to comfort her.

"Has he hurt you, baby?" Clint's heart beat a million miles an hour.

"No, but the ropes are too tight," she cried. "I don't like it here. I want to go home with you, Daddy."

"You've got your proof of life," Wayne said, replacing Emily's voice.

"Damn you, Gossage. Let Emily go. She's just a baby," Clint cried.

"She stays here with me," Gossage replied.

"What about Lizzy? I also need to know that she's okay, too," Clint said.

There was another moment of silence. "Clint, we're in an abandoned house," Lizzy said quickly and then there was the sound of a slap. Lizzy cried out and Emily screamed.

And then the line went dead.

Chapter 13

"We need to search every abandoned house in the area," Clint said in a fever pitch. The sound of the slap... Lizzy's cry and Emily's scream all whirled around in his head in a sickening crescendo that made him feel half crazed.

"You all don't realize just how evil this man is. The threats he's made against Emily were vile and disgusting." A sob escaped him. "We've got to find them now, before he follows through on those threats." God, he hoped it wasn't too late. He hoped Wayne hadn't touched his baby girl in any way.

"We need to have a plan," Derrick Larans, one of the FBI agents, said. "If we show up at the right abandoned house without a plan, then people could be killed."

"Then, make a damned plan," Clint snapped. He drew in a deep breath to control himself. "Sorry, I don't mean to yell at you."

"It's fine," Dallas said. "I'm surprised you haven't snapped before now. I don't want this information about abandoned houses to get out to any of the other searchers. The last thing I want is for a group of town people to stumble on this, and then things could explode in a way none of us want."

"Maybe you need to call off the search except for your officers and us," Derrick said.

"How long is all this going to take?" Clint asked in frustration. "Every single minute counts now. We know they're alive right now, but that could change in the blink of an eye."

"It won't take long, but I'd rather take a few minutes now and get it right rather than rush it and have a tragedy on our hands," Dallas replied. He then got on his radio and called in all of his officers.

Once again, Clint paced the floor. At least now they had a clue, but he didn't even want to think about what price Lizzy might had paid for blurting out the particular piece of information about them being held in an abandoned house. He'd heard a slap, but how many more had followed?

The officers began to trickle in, and thankfully, Walt also returned so Dallas was able to tell the man the search was called off. "We need all the townspeople to stand down right now," Dallas said to the older man. "It's important, Walt. You need to call them all off."

"I'll take care of it," Walt assured them.

"How many abandoned houses are there in the area," Clint asked once Walt had left the house.

"Maybe ten or twelve," Dallas said.

Before any plans could be made for the new search, Clint's phone rang.

He snatched it up and hit the speaker button. "I'm looking forward to meeting you again in person," Wayne said.

"I'm definitely looking forward to it," Clint replied. "Just tell me where you are and we can make that happen."

"We'll plan to meet at five o'clock this evening. I'll tell you the directions to where I am when it gets closer to that time. You come alone, Joe. If I see a cop, then Emily and Lizzy die. If I smell a cop, the two die in a particularly delicious manner. You come alone and unarmed and maybe we can figure out a way that the two females survive. Got it?"

"Got it," Clint replied.

The phone immediately went dead.

"I'll go in alone," Clint said. "I'm the one he wants to kill. Hopefully before that happens, I'll be able to get him to release Lizzy and Emily."

"I'm not letting you sacrifice yourself, Clint," Dallas replied. "My men can find shadows to hide in. They can move without being detected. Once we know the location, they can get into a position to take this guy down, and hopefully nobody has to die."

A large lump of anxiety filled Clint's chest. Could Dallas's men really do what Dallas said they could? Could they back him up without being seen? Clint's biggest fear was that he'd walk into that abandoned house to find that Lizzy and Emily were already dead. And yet he knew that would take away some of Wayne's fun. It was obvious Wayne wanted him to watch the two females die.

He glanced at the clock that hung on the kitchen wall. It was one o'clock. He had four long hours to wait. "I don't want any further searches to be done until I hear from Wayne again," he said. "I don't want any officers stumbling on this house until we see if Wayne really gives me the directions to the place."

"Surely your officers could go in like ghosts to search some of these places now," Derrick said to Dallas.

"I don't want that," Clint protested vehemently. All it would take was one single mistake and Wayne would kill Lizzy and Emily without thinking twice about it. "I want everyone to wait before any more searching is done."

"I tend to agree with you, Clint," Dallas replied. "I think we all should pause and rest up before five o'clock. I know everyone is exhausted and we don't want tiredness to be the reason for a mistake."

Most of the men had worked throughout the night. Dallas looked beyond tired and Clint knew he himself looked haggard from lack of sleep and worry. Not that he cared how he looked. How could he sleep when the two people he loved most in the world were being held by a vicious serial killer? He couldn't believe they were all waiting for instructions from Gossage, but that's exactly what they were doing.

Within an hour, officers were sprawled all over his house. Two napped on the sofa and one was asleep in his chair. There were two more in his bedroom and another two in his guest room.

Thankfully, nobody had entered Emily's room. Clint went back there now and returned to the rocking chair. He closed his eyes and thought about his daughter.

She had literally saved his life. When Samantha had been murdered, it had been the two-year-old little girl who had forced him to grieve quickly and then get on with the task of being a single father.

Without Emily, he would have drowned in his own grief. He might have turned to drugs or alcohol to cope with his devastating loss.

Then now there was Lizzy, who had made him realize he could love again. And now, if she got out of this alive, she would probably hate him forever. Not only had he lied to her about who he was, but by loving her, he'd brought this monstrous danger and the vile killer to her life.

At some point he must have dozed off because he came to with a jolt. His heart beat a frantic pace. What time was it? Had he slept so long he'd missed the call? He jumped up off the rocker and walked through the living room and into the kitchen. His gaze shot to the clock. Thank God it was only three thirty.

Dallas sat at the table with a cup of coffee. "Join me?"

"Sure." Clint grabbed a cup and filled it with what smelled like fresh brew. He then sank down across from Dallas.

"Long day," Dallas said.

"The longest day of my life," Clint replied. He took a sip of the coffee. "I thought the murder of my wife was the worst thing that could ever happen to me, but this...this nightmare is far worse."

"You should have told me," Dallas replied softly. "You should have come to me when you first moved to town and told me you were in the witness protection program."

"Maybe I should have, but somehow I don't think that would have changed the way things have played out."

"What I don't understand is how this guy has stayed under the radar. We're a townspeople who usually notices if there's a stranger among us."

"I wouldn't know who's a stranger and who isn't," Clint replied. Clint frowned as a sudden thought jumped into his head. "Lizzy recently hired two new ranch hands. She mentioned that one of them was new to the area. His name is Tristen, uh, damn, I can't remember his last name."

Clint's heart squeezed tight. He'd never seen Tristen in person. Was it possible Tristen was Wayne? Working next door, he would have been able to see the comings and goings at Clint's place. Had he been that close all along? The idea brought a new sickness to Clint's soul. He would have immediately recognized Wayne if he'd actually seen the ranch hand in person.

"I never met anyone named Tristen before," Dallas replied.

"I think it's very possible Wayne is Tristen, not that it really matters anymore." Clint took another drink of the coffee. "I hope we didn't make a mistake calling things off for the last couple of hours."

"Yeah, me, too," Dallas replied. "It went against everything I've ever known in law enforcement. But it really sounded like the best way for us to operate. Now let's just hope Gossage calls and gives you directions to where they're holed up."

At four o'clock Dallas got all his men up and made sure they were fully alert. A thick tension filled the air as the minutes slowly ticked by.

Clint's biggest fear was that Wayne wouldn't call and they would have lost all of the afternoon resting when they could have been out searching. His hope was that he would finally come face-to-face with the man who featured in his nightmares and he'd be able to talk him into letting the other two go unharmed.

Finally, at a quarter till five, Clint's phone rang. "Go north on Main Street until you leave town," Wayne instructed without preamble. "Go about a mile and then turn right on Locust Street. Take Locust until you come to Oak. Make a right on Oak and take it until you come to K Highway. The house is on the corner lot of K and Oak. Remember, no cops. If I see a cop, then somebody dies. Come alone and unarmed. We'll be waiting for you." He disconnected.

"I know that place," Dallas said. "It's the old Meuller place. It's on a thick, wooded lot that's overgrown, which should make it easier for all of us," he said to his men.

"Are you sure about this?" Clint asked. The last thing he wanted was the cops to make a mistake. A single mistake by them could mean life or death.

"Positive, I trust my men completely and there's no way I want you to walk in that house without plenty of backup," Dallas replied. "However, I don't need all of the men to go." He called off five names. "Between the six of us, we should be able to handle this."

"Where are the FBI agents?" Clint asked, realizing the two were missing.

"They went back to their motel room to rest and haven't come back yet," Dallas replied. "We can handle this without them. I don't need those two to screw things up. I know what I'm doing."

"Then, let's go," Clint said. His blood burned with the need to get this all over with. He would gladly give up his own life for his daughter. He would also do the same for Lizzy. It was time for him to see if he could actually bargain with the devil.

Minutes later he was in his truck and headed into town. His hands were slick with perspiration as a sick anxiety rolled around in his stomach. He glanced up in his rearview mirror and saw Dallas not far behind him. Thankfully they had managed to commandeer two other cars that were not patrol cars. So, to any onlooker, there were no cops in sight.

He had no idea what he would be facing when he walked into the abandoned house. But he presumed it would be his own death. He just hoped Lizzy walked away alive and would take in Emily as her daughter. He knew Lizzy would be a loving, caring mother to Emily. He knew his beautiful daughter would thrive under her care.

He also knew he probably wouldn't be killed the minute he got into the door. Wayne would want to see him squirm. The man would want to remind Clint of how much smarter he was than all the people in town. He would want to crow at his success in pulling all this off.

As he reached the opposite side of town, he slowed down, unsure where Locust Street was. Dallas's car, and the car following Dallas both sped around him. They went a little farther and then both of the cars in front of him slowed down and turned on their right blinkers.

However, they didn't turn, even though the street was Locust Street. Instead, they sped ahead and Clint turned right. He wondered if he would ever see Dallas or any of the other men again.

Please let them be alive and unharmed. The words repeated themselves over and over again in his mind as he thought of Emily and Lizzy. It was a mantra that refused to stop playing as he got closer and closer to his destination.

If he got the opportunity, he'd take Gossage down. If he got the chance, he'd gladly kill the man. He tightened his fingers around the steering wheel, imagining they were wrapped around Gossage's neck. He would gladly kill the man and not feel bad about it at all.

The road he was traveling on was narrow, with fields on either side and tall trees encroaching on the pavement. He felt as if he was in the middle of nowhere.

He drove slowly for several more miles, looking for Oak. When he finally reached it, it was another narrow, desolate road with plenty of trees and fields of both corn and wheat on either side.

He continued on and then he saw it. The abandoned house at the corner of Oak and K Highway. He turned into the house's driveway, which was overgrown with weeds and brush. He cut his engine and took a moment to look around the area as his heartbeat raced in his chest.

Were Dallas and his men already somewhere out here? He gazed around, but there was nobody in sight. If they were here, then Dallas was right, they were good at blending in and finding hidey-holes.

He turned his attention to the front door and drew

in several deep breaths for courage, for the strength to deal with whatever he would face once he walked in.

The place looked deserted, with a front porch that listed to the left and steps up that were half-broken. Faded, old and dirty beige paint covered the structure. There was no vehicle to be seen. Was this the right house? It had to be.

With his nerves ringing loudly throughout his body and a fight or flight adrenaline filling him, he cut his truck engine. Drawing another couple of deep breaths, he then stepped out of his truck. What would he see when he opened the front door?

Please let them be alive and unharmed. The mantra began once again in his head as he headed to the rickety porch. Dallas had wanted him to come in with a gun, but Clint had refused. The last thing he wanted was for Wayne to find a weapon on him and then in his anger over it he harmed one or both of his captives.

With another deep breath, Clint reached the front door and after a moment of hesitation, he opened it. He stepped into a small living room with a broken-down recliner chair as the only furnishing.

The very air inside smelled old and abandoned. It reeked of staleness and dust with a faint odor of something decaying. He heard nothing and saw nobody.

"Hello?" he called out.

"We're waiting for you in here," Wayne's voice replied from what Clint assumed was the kitchen. Clint followed the voice and the first thing he saw was Lizzy and Emily tied to two straight-backed chairs.

"Daddy!" Emily yelled at the sight of him and then began to cry. "Daddy, please, untie me and take me home. Take me home, Daddy."

His first instinct was to run to his daughter, but before he could even take a step toward her, a gun barrel pressed hard into the center of his back. "Welcome to your nightmare," Wayne said. "I hope you don't mind, but I need to know that you came in here clean. If you even flinch while I search you then I'll put a bullet in your daughter's forehead."

He proceeded to do a thorough pat down, making Clint grateful he hadn't tried to sneak a gun in. When the pat down was over, Wayne motioned him to a third kitchen chair that faced Lizzy and Emily.

For the first time Clint really looked at his lover and his daughter. One of Lizzy's cheeks was bright red and he suspected it was due to the slap he'd heard over the phone. She must have been slapped more than once for her cheek to be so enflamed. Emily's eyes were swollen, but he believed it was due to her crying.

Thank God that for the most part, they both looked relatively okay. "Let them go," he said to Wayne. "They have nothing to do with this. I'm the one you want. This is strictly between you and me."

Gossage looked different than he'd looked years ago. His face was leaner and he had a neat, black beard covering the lower part of his jaw. "I'm telling you, Gossage, they aren't important."

"They are important to this, because I want you to watch them die before I kill you," Wayne shouted.

"Dammit, they aren't important. This is between you and me," Clint repeated with fervor.

Wayne laughed, the deep sound of the devil's mirth. "Excuse me, but you aren't the one in charge of what happens next. If you move from that chair, then I'll shoot your daughter."

Wayne stood in front of him and smiled. "Do you want me to tell you all the wonderful ways I'm going to hurt them before I shoot you?"

"I don't think that's necessary," Clint replied as he tried to figure out how he could get the upper hand. Already he felt a rage building inside him, but he knew he had to keep his wits and couldn't succumb to the rage.

Wayne walked over to Lizzy and stroked a length of her blond hair. Lizzy tossed her head as if to evade his touch. Wayne laughed and grabbed her hair, pulling it until Lizzy winced with pain.

Clint half rose from the chair, and then Wayne pointed his gun at Emily and Clint sank back down. But his anger seethed inside of him, bordering on a rage he'd never felt before in his life.

"Oh, this is going to be such fun," Gossage said. He then punched Lizzy in the stomach and Clint saw red. No longer thinking, but acting on his rage, he leaped out of the chair and barreled toward the monster that had reentered his life.

A shot rang out at the same time Clint made contact with Wayne's body. Wayne fell to the floor on his back and Clint jumped on top of him. Clint pounded him in the face as Wayne tried to get up or, at the very least, evade Clint's fist. Wayne tried to reach out for the gun that had fallen out of his hand and now lay just outside his reach.

"You bastard," Clint yelled as he continued to hit the man. "You sick bastard." At that moment, Dallas and his men rushed in. "Enough, Clint," he said. "Get off him now." He pulled Clint off Wayne.

As Clint's brain began to work again, he frantically looked over at his daughter, who was sobbing, but she didn't appear to have been shot. He then gazed at Lizzy, who was crying, too, but also appeared to be okay.

It was over. Finally the nightmare was over and he and Emily could resume their normal lives. But would it be with Lizzy in it or not? Or would she be unable to forgive him for his lies and this horror that he'd brought into her life?

It seemed like it took forever for Lizzy to be untied, and then she was placed on a gurney and taken to an awaiting ambulance. There was a second ambulance there to take Emily into the hospital as well.

They'd had no food or water since they'd been taken, but aside from an aching stomach where Wayne had hit her, a burning cheek where he'd slapped her several times, and the burning of her raw wrists, she felt relatively okay.

She was also overwhelmed with everything that had happened. As Dallas had untied her, he'd told her that Clint had been in the witness protection program. The news had stunned her and made her wonder what was real and what had only been pretend between them.

Two hours later she was in a bed in a hospital room. She had been allowed to shower and change into a hospital gown. The doctor wanted her to stay for at least one night. She was receiving fluids intravenously and had eaten a small, light meal.

She felt numb, as if too much information had made her brain stop working. Dallas had filled her in on so much of what had happened in Clint's past. She just couldn't digest it all. She was too tired and too stressed with the trauma she'd just endured to process anything else.

Bailey was the first person to show up in her room. "I turn my back on you for one minute and look what kind of trouble you get in," she said as she sat at the foot of Lizzy's bed.

Lizzy opened her mouth to lightly quip back to her friend, but to her horror, she began to cry. All of her deep emotions exploded out of her in tears.

"Oh, girlfriend." Bailey said softly and she instantly moved to pull Lizzy into her arms. As Lizzy cried, Bailey also cried. The two sobbed together for several minutes and then they managed to get themselves under control.

Bailey moved to the chair next to Lizzy's bed. "Are you sure you're okay? Are you hurt?" Bailey asked worriedly.

"Not really. My face still stings where I got slapped a couple of times and my wrists hurt from where I tried to get out of the ropes, but other than that, I'm okay. The main thing is that Emily is okay," Lizzy replied.

"I was so scared for you, Lizzy. I can't believe what happened to you. The whole town is buzzing about it. I was sick with worry about you. How are you and Clint? Have you had a chance to talk to him yet?"

"There is no 'me and Clint.' I don't even know what to think where he's concerned. Clint isn't even his true name. I don't know what was real and what wasn't with him." Tears threatened to fall once again as she thought of the man she loved. Had he truly cared for her at all or had he merely needed her to help him fit into his life on the ranch? He'd even lied about his late wife. She hadn't been a drug addict at all. She'd been the victim of Tristen, who was a vicious serial killer.

"Bailey, I appreciate you stopping by, but I'm really exhausted," Lizzy finally said.

"Oh, of course." Bailey stood. "I just needed to see for myself that you were okay."

"I will be," Lizzy replied. The two said their goodbyes and then Lizzy lowered the head of her bed and closed her eyes. She didn't really feel like talking to anyone right now. She also didn't want to replay the horror of being tied up and not knowing if or when she'd be killed…if or when little Emily might be killed.

All she really wanted now was the sweet oblivion of sleep. There had been too much information about Clint, slapping her in the face. There were just too many emotions shifting through her for her to sort out tonight. They would all be there waiting for her the next morning, and maybe after a good night's sleep, she would be better prepared to deal with everything.

The next time she awakened it was to the morning sun creeping in through her window. All she wanted now was to go home. She wanted her own things surrounding her. She desperately needed the familiarity of her own place right now. She hoped the doctor let her go within the next couple of hours.

At least she'd slept without dreams. She'd been afraid she might have terrible nightmares about the trauma she'd endured, but thankfully she hadn't. She wondered if she would see Clint today.

Her heart squeezed tight at the mere thought of him. Would he even want to see her? At this point she wasn't sure how to feel about him. And she couldn't even begin to think of how he might really feel about her. She couldn't think about him right now.

Within two hours she'd had breakfast and the doctor had been in to see her. He'd agreed to release her since she had no real wounds other than her wrists, which would heal up over time.

She called Bailey for a ride, and twenty minutes later, she was in Bailey's car and headed home. "I know your truck is parked at Clint's place. Do you want me to take you there to get it?" Bailey asked.

"No, I'll get it in a day or two. I'm not planning on leaving my house for the next couple of days anyway."

"Are you going to be okay, here in the house, all alone?" Bailey asked. "You know I could stay with you if you need me to."

Lizzy shot a warm look at her friend. "Thanks, Bailey, but I'll be fine."

In truth, she wanted to be alone. She didn't want to have to put on a brave front for anyone. If she wanted to cry, she wanted the privacy to really ugly cry. If she wanted to scream, then she could scream out all the emotions that still whirled around in her head.

Bailey pulled up in front of Lizzy's place, and after goodbyes were said, Lizzy walked to the front door. Her purse with her keys were at Clint's. Thankfully she kept a spare house key behind one of the two lights on the garage.

She retrieved it now and unlocked the door and then closed and locked it behind her. She tossed the key on an end table and then collapsed on the sofa.

She was still both mentally and physically exhausted by the ordeal she'd gone through. She'd been so afraid for herself, but she'd been absolutely terrified for little Emily.

Wayne had enjoyed scaring them with what he intended to do to them once Clint arrived. His words had been evil and twisted and she hoped Emily never, ever heard those kinds of words again for the rest of her life. She also hoped the little girl would be able to put this all behind her and not hang on to any trauma.

For the next two days Lizzy slept and ate. She cried and tried to center herself after all she'd been through. She received a beautiful bouquet of flowers from the city council and Elijah stopped by from the food pantry and brought her a cake that Harper had donated from her bakery.

The person who didn't call or come by to see her was Clint. As far as she was concerned, it was a sign that he was done with her. That it had never been real between them.

That was the death she mourned. That was the reason for her ugly crying. She'd thought she'd found her Mr. Perfect and he had only been mirage. It had been so real for her, but apparently it had not been for him.

By the third day of silence from him, an anger started to build up in her. She wasn't angry with him about the ordeal she had suffered at the hands of his serial killer. He'd had no idea that his monster was so close. Heck, she'd hired the damned monster as one of her ranch hands. No, she didn't blame Clint for any of that.

She was angry, because at the very least, she deserved him looking her in the eye and admitting that he'd lied to her about so many things. At the very least she deserved a phone call from him to check in on how she was doing. She now didn't know exactly who she'd fallen in love with.

She thought of all the ways she'd helped him, making it so much easier for him to fit into his new life. Had he just used her? Had he pretended to care about her when all he was doing was using her for her knowledge and for all the connections she had in the small town?

The more she thought about it, the angrier she got. She deserved some kind of explanation from him. On the fourth day of being home with no word from him, it was just afternoon when she left her house to walk next door.

At the very least, she needed to get her purse and her truck. She hoped to also have a conversation with him where she could express her anger at him. It was Wednesday, so Emily should be back in school and she would be able to express herself without restraint.

She walked briskly. The slight cool breeze held the scents of autumn…of fireplace smoke and ripened apples and dying leaves. With each step she took, her heart beat faster and an anxiety built up, along with the anger inside her.

The fact that he hadn't tried to contact her in the time that had passed since she'd left the hospital told her that the relationship had never been real and that it was over between them. The silence from him let her know that he'd merely used her to gain acceptance in the community.

When she reached his place, she knocked on the door with more force than she intended. He opened the door and he'd never looked more handsome to her, although his eyes held a slightly haunted look.

"Lizzy," he said and smiled at her. It was the smile that had always warmed her and touched her heart. "I'm so glad you're here."

"Hi, Clint...or should I say Joe? I've just come to get my purse and my truck," she replied stiffly, her anger simmering just beneath the surface, inside her.

His smile faded. "Lizzy, I know you must hate me right now for putting your life in danger, but could you come in and let me explain some things?"

"I'm not sure we have anything to talk about," she replied and averted her gaze from his.

"I have so much to talk to you about," he said.

"You certainly haven't been in any hurry to speak to me," she replied, her anger rife in her tone.

"Lizzy, please come in."

She made the mistake of looking up into his eyes. There appeared to be a genuine plea there. "Okay," she said after a moment of hesitation. He led her into the living room where she sat on one end of the sofa and he sat on the other. "How's Emily?" she asked,

"She's doing okay, considering everything she's been through. She's been pretty clingy to me for the last few days, but she was eager to go back to school this morning. I want to thank you for being so strong for her. She told me how you talked to her and told her stories whenever you could."

"I just wanted to soothe her fears as best as I was able. And by the way, I don't hate you for the way things went down with Wayne Lee Gossage."

"I was afraid you did and that's why I haven't contacted you. I figured if you wanted to see me or talk to me again, you'd let me know." His gaze searched her features, as if looking for answers. "But you are angry with me," he surmised.

"I am. First of all, I'm angry that you haven't even called me to see how I was doing. I went through a lot and yet you haven't checked on me to make sure I was doing okay."

"When I was at the hospital, I did check in with your doctor to make sure you were physically all right. Lizzy, I wanted to call you every day. I wanted to go over and see you, but I thought you might not welcome me. I figured I'd let you take the lead, because I really thought you would hate me for putting your very life at risk."

"I told you I'm not angry about that. You couldn't know that your daughter and I would be kidnapped by the madman from your past. I'm angry because I don't really know who you are. You lied to me about so many things I don't even know what to believe," she said with frustration.

"Lizzy, I might have lied about a lot of things in

order to keep my cover, but the one thing I didn't lie about was my feelings for you."

He leaned toward her and took one of her hands in his. "No matter what my name is, I'm in love with you, Lizzy. No matter what my background is, I'm desperately in love with you, Lizzy, and that's something I would never lie about."

She pulled her hand from his. She'd wanted him to love her and she'd longed to hear the very words he'd just spoken. But right now, it didn't feel quite right. She couldn't say the words back to him.

"Maybe we just need to start all over again," she finally said. "I need to get to know Joe instead of Clint."

"We're the same man, Lizzy. Strip away the name and what lies I said to keep my cover in place, and my heart still knows what it wants and it wants you." His eyes implored her to understand, to accept him.

Her anger toward him was gone, but she still didn't feel quite ready to jump headfirst back to where they had been. "I still say I need to get to know Joe better." She stood, feeling tears pressing hot against her eyes.

What in the heck was wrong with her? "If I could just get my purse, then I'll get out of here for now."

"Of course, I'll go get your purse from where I put it in the kitchen." He returned a moment later with the item in hand. "Think about what I said, Lizzy, but if you feel better in starting over, then I'm willing to do that. Whatever it takes to win your love, that's what I want to do."

"Thanks, Clint... I mean, Joe." Unexpected tears threatened to fall, but she managed to leave his house before he saw them.

Once she was back in her house and again on her sofa, her tears dried up as she found herself wondering for the second time what was wrong with her?

The truth of the matter was she was afraid to believe him. She was afraid to accept his words of love, in case they weren't real. Yet why wouldn't they be real? What reason did he have to lie to her now?

Had she just pushed away the love of her life for nothing? Would Clint... Joe even want to pursue her anymore now that she hadn't told him that she loved him, too? Now she wished she would have told him. She wished that she had just accepted that he loved her.

She finally decided it was time to stop thinking and do something physical. Thankfully Rory had kept things running smoothly at the ranch while she'd been out of commission. But it was time she checked things out for herself. For the past four days she'd been wallowing in her feelings. Now it was time she got back to the world of the living.

Before she could head outside, a knock fell on her door. Maybe it was another well-wisher. She pulled open her door to see Clint... Joe standing there. He swept a black cowboy hat off his head and smiled at her.

"Howdy, ma'am. My name is Joe Masterson. Me and my young daughter, Emily, just moved in next door and I was wondering if you'd like to come to the café with us this evening so we can get to know each other better."

She stared at him, and in that moment, all the love she had for him flooded through her. She took his hand and pulled him over the threshold and into the house and then she wrapped her arms around his neck.

"I'd love to have dinner this evening with you and your daughter," she replied. "I'd love to eat lots and lots of dinners with you, because no matter what your name is, I love you madly."

His entire face lit up. "Lizzy, really, you do?"

"I do," she replied.

"Oh, Lizzy, those are two words I'd love to hear you say in front of a preacher as soon as possible, because I want you to be my wife forever and always. I want you to be a mother to Emily, who already loves you so much."

"I would love to be your wife and a mother to Emily, who I love dearly. I think we're going to make Emily very happy." Before she could say another word, his mouth took hers in a kiss that solidified her feelings for him.

There was no way she believed a man who was merely playing with her heart could kiss her with such longing and love. There was nothing false in his kiss, and she now knew she was going to have a wonderful life with the cowboy next door.

* * *

The Scarecrow Killer sat in his basement. He'd been angry for the past three days. Each day the newspaper had run with headlines about the pathetic serial killer who had come in from New York and encroached on his territory.

The Nighttime Creeper… What a stupid name. It made the man sound like some kind of a slug that slithered across the pavement. Whenever the Scarecrow Killer saw a slug, he liked to pour salt on it and then watch it writhe in agony until its death.

Thank God the serial killer had been arrested and taken back to New York where he'd be in prison for the rest of his days. He had a feeling the man wouldn't be escaping again anytime soon.

But it was time for the Scarecrow Killer to claim the front page of the paper again. He didn't want the people of Millsville to forget about him.

He looked over to his stash of goodies. There were poles and old hats and clothes to dress up his next victim. Then, there was the black thread he used to sew up the mouths and the surgical tools he needed to take their eyes.

He looked over to the shelf where two sets of eyeballs looked back at him. A wild excitement swept through him. Oh yes, it was definitely time for him to be on the front page of the paper again, and the way to do that was to take another victim and turn them into a human scarecrow.

He laughed, the sound echoing off the concrete walls. It was time… It was past time for the Scarecrow Killer to kill again.

* * * * *

Don't miss Carla Cassidy's previous title in
The Scarecrow Murders:

Guarding a Forbidden Love
Killer in the Heartland
Other titles include:
The Last Cowboy Standing
The Cowboy's Targeted Bride
Cowboy's Vow to Protect

Available now from
Harlequin Romantic Suspense

For a sneak peek at the next
Coltons of New York story,
Protecting Colton's Secret Daughters
by Lisa Childs, turn the page...

Chapter 1

Since the killings had begun, FBI special agent Cash Colton had spent more time at the Manhattan field office than he had anywhere else, so it felt strange to be outside now. Well, inside an SUV driving toward Coney Island, but it wasn't the office or a crime scene, which was the only other place he'd been besides the office.

At least Coney Island wasn't a crime scene yet. But after the text he'd received, the text that haunted him, Cash couldn't help fearing that he might be heading to another crime scene soon and not just because of the way that killer kept killing. That fear, because of that damn text, compelled him to make the trip to Coney Island, to make sure *she* was okay.

Even before receiving that text, he'd been as determined as the rest of his special unit to catch the Landmark serial killer. The first victim, Mark Weldon, had been shot in Central Park and found with a typed note stuffed in his pocket: *Until the brilliant and beautiful Maeve O'Leary is freed, I will kill in her honor and name. M down, A up next.*

Like this lunatic could actually expect them to free a serial killer because of his threats? Then there would be two serial killers terrorizing New York, although Maeve hadn't limited her killing just to the Empire State. She'd killed wherever and whomever she'd married. She'd also tried to kill a lover's wife in order to inherit that woman's fortune. Anything for money...

Insatiable greed was Maeve's motive for murder.

Why was the Landmark Killer killing? What was his motive? Had Maeve somehow brainwashed him like she had that poor psychiatrist? Like she had all her husbands?

But even she had to see that there was no way she was getting released; she wasn't even going to get bail after the murders she'd committed.

That hadn't stopped her admirer, though. The Landmark Killer's second victim, Andrew Copowski, had been found on the Empire State Building observation deck with a typed note in his pocket. It had read nearly the same as the first, but the second line said, *MA down, E up.*

The next attempt had been on Broadway but that

victim had fortunately survived. Unfortunately, since his assailant had worn a mask and a hoodie, he hadn't been able to provide much more than a vague description. Male, maybe on the younger side...

It wasn't much, but along with the other notes, not the ones left in the pockets of the victims but the personal texts the killer had sent, Cash and his team knew the killer was probably closer than they'd realized. Closer to them than they were to finding him.

He had to be stopped, before anyone else died, and before anyone else was threatened. Like Valentina had been threatened...

Maybe not specifically but the threat had been implied in the text Cash had received; he was the latest one singled out on the FBI serial-killer team. His twin had been the first to be taunted.

Who the hell was it? Was it someone close to them like they had come to suspect? Someone within the FBI or within the 98th Precinct who had worked to hunt down the Black Widow serial killer, Maeve O'Leary? Someone who'd come to admire her for some sick reason?

The note about Valentina had been a text sent to Cash's phone after the first victim had been shot on Broadway. No worries. Lots where that dippy actor came from. Tsk-tsk, Cash—murdered Daddy and a sad ex-wife.

Instead of trying for another actor, the killer had claimed the life of an assistant theater director after that text. And what about Valentina?

Was she in danger? Had that text been meant as an actual threat or was it just a ploy to distract Cash from the case? While it likely was a ploy, Cash wasn't immune to the text. It had worked. He was distracted. He couldn't stop worrying about Valentina even though he'd told a friend at the local police precinct about the note and had asked Officer Dave Powers to watch out for her, to make sure that nobody was lurking around her, trying to hurt her.

Was she really sad?

Why?

She couldn't still be unhappy about their divorce. More than three years had passed since Cash had set her free to have what she'd really wanted: a husband who wasn't consumed with his work, and most especially children. More than anything else, more than him, Valentina had wanted a family.

Because Cash hadn't been able to see how he could handle his career, marriage and fatherhood, he'd done what he'd thought would make Valentina the happiest. After she'd moved out to get some space from him, he'd filed for divorce. He'd wanted her to have the happiness she deserved. So why wasn't she happy? Or was the texter lying about that?

He hadn't lied about Cash's murdered daddy. That had happened, and a serial killer was responsible for Cash's cop father losing his life.

And inadvertently responsible for Cash and all his siblings going into law enforcement.

So since he'd told the truth about that, he might

have about Valentina as well. But how would the Landmark Killer know if Cash's ex-wife was happy or sad unless he'd gotten close to her? Did he know her? Or had he been stalking her like he had his victims?

Those worries kept Cash awake at night, kept him on edge. Even though he'd asked his buddy at the local precinct to keep an eye on her, Cash had also called Valentina to let her know about that text. To make sure she was aware of the potential threat. She'd been short with him, as if he'd caught her at a bad time. And maybe he had…

And ever since he'd heard her voice, he hadn't been able to get it out of his mind. Just as he'd never gotten Valentina Acosta completely out of his heart. Cash suspected that the Landmark Killer had known that when he'd sent Cash the text. He'd known how badly it would bother him, so somehow he knew Cash.

Maybe better than Cash knew himself because in the past three years he hadn't let himself admit to how he felt about Valentina. He rarely let himself think about her at all. If not for that damn text…

And then that call he'd made to her, to the same cell number she'd always had. Brennan had offered to make the call for him, as if it was somehow his fault that Cash had received the text even though their entire unit was hunting this sick serial killer. But he'd sent Brennan the first text: Shouldn't you be

out looking for me skulking around Broadway the-
aters instead of shacking up with a murder suspect?I
thought you Coltons didn't like killers because of
what happened to poor Daddy.

Brennan had been reluctant to share the text with
them. Probably because of the shacking-up part.
Cash smiled and caught a glimpse of his own reflection in the rearview mirror. Despite being twins,
he and Brennan looked nothing alike because they
were fraternal, not identical. Brennan had pale blond
hair and pale blue eyes and a baby face, while Cash
had brown hair, green eyes and always looked like
he needed a shave even if he'd just shaved. But given
how busy he was, he'd given up and wore a beard
now.

Valentina had always told him that she thought
his scruff was sexy. But that was when he'd kept his
beard nearly trimmed. He didn't look neat now. He
probably should have stopped at home and showered
after leaving the office, but for some reason he'd had
this compulsion to drive to Brooklyn and Coney Island. To see for himself that Valentina was really all
right, that she was safe and not sad.

"Valentina? Are you all right?"

The voice startled her, drawing her attention back
to the present, and not the past, where it had been
constantly slipping since that call a week ago. From
Cash...

She had not heard the sound of his deep voice

in three years, but she'd immediately recognized the rumble of it in her ear, goose bumps rising on her skin then like they were rising now despite the warmth of the library.

Valentina... he'd murmured.

"Valentina!" an older woman repeated again. "Are you all right?"

She shook her head and blinked and squinted against the late-afternoon sun pouring through the tall windows. Then she tried to focus on the woman standing in front of her, blocking her path, as Valentina had tried to push the double stroller between the rows of children's books.

"You're not all right," Mrs. Miller remarked, and she reached over the top of the stroller to pat Valentina's hand. "What's troubling you, honey?" The back of the woman's hand had thick veins crisscrossing it, and on every finger, below the swollen knuckle, she wore a ring with big stones that sparkled and reflected back the sunlight. The sun also glinted off the jewels hanging from the chains around her neck, too.

Four pudgy little hands stretched out from the stroller, reaching toward those shiny pendants. The girls loved shiny things.

Valentina smiled. "Nothing, Mrs. Miller. I'm fine. Really."

The woman stepped back then and leaned down to smile at the toddlers in the stroller. "How could you not be happy all the time with these two gorgeous girls?"

Mother's pride suffused Valentina. "I just picked them up from day care." If they didn't love going to school, as they called it, she might have regretted having to work full-time. But as a single mother, she didn't have a choice. At least she had a job that she enjoyed.

"And you came right back to work?" Mrs. Miller asked with surprise.

"We're picking out a book for bedtime. Well, two books. They each get to choose one."

"You're passing your librarian's love for books on to your little girls—that's wonderful," Mrs. Miller enthused. "And speaking of books..."

"I tracked down that memoir you've been looking for," Valentina assured her.

"That's wonderful!" the woman exclaimed, her pale blue eyes sparkling like her rings with excitement.

"I ordered it to be sent here from the branch where I found it. If it arrives while I'm off this weekend, I asked Randall to call you and let you know if it gets here before Monday," Valentina said.

"I can wait until you're back on Monday, honey," the woman said. "Then you and I can discuss it."

That was one of the parts of Valentina's job that she enjoyed most. Discussing books with other avid readers.

The older woman loved reading the memoirs of famous theater actors and actresses and socialites and artists from years past, probably looking for a mention of herself. She'd once been an actress before marrying well and becoming a socialite; there was even a rumor that she had also been a famous artist's model and muse.

"When are you going to write your memoir?" Valentina asked. "Yours is the book I would love to read."

The older woman blushed and giggled and waved a hand in front of her face, and the sunlight glinted off all of the bright stones on her rings. She had that air about her, with the furs she wore and her perfect makeup and clothes and jewelry, of old Hollywood glamour. "I might be scribbling down a few notes here and there," she admitted with a sly smile. "But I find myself focusing on other things and events more than myself. I'm definitely not the type to kiss and tell. But I certainly enjoy reading the stories from the people who do."

Valentina laughed now, and the girls echoed it, despite having no idea what she was laughing about.

Mrs. Miller giggled again, and she looked much younger than her probably eighty or ninety years. "You enjoy your bedtime stories," she told them, and she patted Valentina's hand again as she walked past them.

The little girls leaned out either side of the stroller and stared after the older woman.

"Sparky..." Luciana murmured.

"Sparky," Ana repeated.

They must have been talking about the older

woman's jewelry. Valentina smiled as her heart filled
with love. They were so adorable with brown curls
framing their little faces. Ana had dark eyes, like
Valentina, while Luci's were green, like…

No. She wasn't going to think about him anymore. And for the next while, she managed that while
helping the girls pick out books. But they knew the
routine, so they chose quickly once they ruled out
the ones they'd already read. Then they checked out
and were back in the stroller, heading toward home,
shortly after Mrs. Miller left.

The distance between the library and the high-rise
condo complex where they lived was far enough that
it was easier and safer to push the girls in their double
stroller than for them to walk. The only problem was
that with the street noise from traffic echoing off the
commercial buildings, Valentina couldn't hear much
of their chatter. Not that she understood much of it;
they had their own little twin language. While they
always understood each other, it wasn't as easy for
Valentina all the time.

She still wasn't certain she understood Cash's call
either. He'd received a text about her from a serial
killer? Or so he and the rest of his unit suspected, but
nobody at the FBI had been able to trace it. With all
their technology, how was that possible?

And why send Cash a text about her?

She had not had any contact with her ex-hus-
band since that day she'd moved out in order to take
some time to think, to figure out if she could accept

what he was willing to give her—whatever time that was left from the job that consumed him. But she'd wanted more than that; she'd wanted a family. And that was the one thing he'd told her he would not give her. But he actually had…

Neither of them had known it when she'd moved out, though. She hadn't even known it when the divorce papers had come. Thinking he didn't care enough to figure out a compromise with her, Valentina had just signed them and ended it without an argument, without a fight. And she'd thought it was done, that she would never see or hear from him again. And she hadn't for three years…

Until that night a week ago.

Valentina…

And just the sound of his deep, rumbly voice had all the feelings rushing back, overwhelmingly intense. The pain, the loss, the guilt…

She should have told him all those years ago when she'd first found out herself that she was pregnant. But she'd figured that it was too late then because she had already signed the divorce papers. And in sending them, Cash had clearly been sending her the message that there was no hope for them as a couple. They were over. Done. He hadn't wanted the same things she had. He certainly hadn't wanted—

A loud pop rang out, startling her and making her jump. It wasn't so much the noise, which must have been a backfiring car that had passed by or started up along the curb or in one of the alleys they'd passed.

It was that she'd been so distracted again that she hadn't even realized where she was. That she had almost walked past the street on which she needed to turn and cross to head home. She had to put that phone call out of her mind.

Cash hadn't called again. And he probably wouldn't. She knew he was busy chasing another killer, like he always was. The Landmark Killer. She'd watched the news and had read the article the *New York Wire* had recently run about the investigation.

No, that article had been more about the investigators than anything else. It had been all about the Coltons, who all worked in the elite serial-killer unit of the FBI. And it had revealed the reason why they were all on that unit and so dedicated to hunting down killers was that a serial killer had murdered their police officer father so many years ago.

But were they hunting the Landmark Killer, or was he hunting them with the notes he left in his victims' pockets and with the text he'd sent Cash?

She didn't know exactly what it had said, just that it had mentioned her. Since she and Cash had had no contact since their divorce, how had this serial killer known about her at all?

Was she in danger? And the girls?

Or were Cash and his siblings really the ones who were in danger and the serial killer was just texting to taunt them like he did with those notes he left on his victims?

* * *

He had killed again.

Like he had so many times before. That didn't even bother him anymore.

Taking a life.

It wasn't a big deal. It was just what he did, like other guys who played video games. But it wasn't a game to him. It was a vocation.

One he had to protect at all costs.

This time he couldn't be certain that he wouldn't get caught. He couldn't be certain unless he *made* certain. He had to eliminate any possibility of being identified as the killer.

So he settled into the driver's seat and pulled the mask over his face and drew up his hood, pulling it tight around that mask so that nothing of his face reflected back at him from the rearview mirror. Nothing but his eyes. His cold, dark eyes.

Chapter 2

Cash knew Valentina's address. She'd given it to him to forward her mail to after she'd moved out of the apartment they'd shared in Manhattan. She'd moved to Coney Island into the condo where her grandparents used to live. Her grandparents, knowing how much their only granddaughter had loved visiting them there, had left the condo to her in their will when they'd passed away shortly before Cash and Valentina's divorce. Valentina had wanted to move out there then, while Cash had wanted to stay close to the Manhattan office.

Maybe losing so much of her family had made Valentina even more desperate to start one of her own. That was when she'd really started pressuring

Cash into having kids, and she'd wanted to raise her children in a place she remembered so fondly from her own childhood. Cash didn't have that many fond memories of his childhood; his father's brutal murder had overshadowed all of the happy ones.

It overshadowed his adulthood, leading him to a life in law enforcement. With his job consuming so much of his time and attention, he shouldn't have become a husband, let alone a father.

Valentina had often told him, during the three years that they'd been married, that she'd felt like a mistress and his career was really his wife. She only got stolen moments of his time, and he'd almost seemed guilty about the time he'd spent with her, the time away from his job. It hadn't been fair to Valentina. She shouldn't have been alone so much while he'd been working. She'd deserved so much more from their marriage, from him. She'd deserved everything she'd wanted.

She was so sweet and loving and smart and beautiful. So very beautiful...

He could see her now in his mind and maybe he even conjured up her image through the side window. Her thick dark hair flowing nearly to her waist, her hips swaying as she walked along the sidewalk. But she was pushing something in front of her. A stroller?

Was she babysitting for a friend?

Or had she started that family she'd wanted with him with someone else? That was what he'd hoped for her when he'd divorced her, but knowing that she had actually moved on with someone else…

And he hadn't. That he was still stuck in their past, dreaming of her smile, of her laugh, of her wicked sense of humor flashing in her dark eyes, and the love…

A car horn tooted behind him and he realized the light had changed to green and the traffic in front of him had moved. But he was still stuck.

He pressed on the accelerator and surged forward through the intersection. The light green at the next one, he drove through that as well because he spied an open parking space ahead on the curb. He was nearly to her condo building. That had to be where she was heading. So he pulled into that spot and hopped out of his SUV. She would be coming this way if she was going home.

But maybe she'd been babysitting for someone and was taking the child back to their parents. Or was she the parent? Had she had the child she wanted? The family?

He wanted to be happy for her. But a part of him had never stopped wanting her…for her. And if that was her he'd seen on the sidewalk, she was every bit as beautiful as she'd always been. As sexy…

His heart pounded hard as he skirted around his SUV and stepped onto the sidewalk. He'd only gotten a couple of blocks ahead of her. She should appear soon, but the sidewalk was packed with people heading toward him, probably intent on enjoying the sunny day at the amusement park or the beach. And her complex was so close to both.

Instead of waiting for her to pass by him, Cash started through the crowd, moving against the throng of people. It had been three years since he'd seen Valentina; maybe that hadn't even been her he'd glimpsed on the sidewalk. Maybe that woman just looked like Valentina with the same curves and the same walk.

But if that woman wasn't his ex-wife, he doubted his heart would be pounding as fast and hard as it was. It wasn't just attraction or anticipation coursing through him, though; it was fear. Something had compelled him to drive out to Coney Island today to make sure she was safe. He'd been worried since he'd received that text, but that worry had intensified, twisting his guts, because he had a sick feeling, almost a premonition, that she was in danger.

He moved faster through the crowd, drawing grunts and curses as he accidentally banged into people. Maybe if they hadn't been on their phones and distracted they would have seen him coming, but he grunted back apologies. Until he neared the next intersection and he saw *her* standing on the other side, then he was the one distracted.

The woman was definitely Valentina. She stood at the curb in front of that stroller, although she was half turned toward it, her hand on top of it as if she was protecting it from the traffic on the street in front of her. The breeze coming in off the ocean played with her hair, swirling the long chocolate-brown tresses around her while plastering her light blue cotton dress against her curves. He knew that body so well that his body tightened with the desire coursing through him. He'd never wanted anyone the way he'd wanted her.

The way he still wanted her...

She didn't see him. Her focus was split between the stroller and the crosswalk light. Once it turned green, she held back a moment, letting other people pass by her. Then, finally, she started across, and just as she did, Cash heard an engine rev, brakes squeal and metal scrape as a car sideswiped the one stopped in front of it to pass it and roar toward the intersection, toward Valentina and that stroller with not one but two children in it.

His heart slammed against his ribs as fear shot through him. He'd been right to worry about her; she was definitely in danger.

Mortal danger...

The asphalt was hard and hot beneath her back. The impact with which Valentina had struck the ground had knocked the breath from her lungs, and she couldn't get it back, not with the heavy weight lying on top of her, pressing her into the ground. Panic gripped her, and now her lungs burned with a scream as well as her lack of breath.

The kids!

The stroller. Had it been knocked over as well? Or had the car done that?

It wasn't the car lying atop Valentina; it was a long, hard body. A familiar body that, even now, after three years, she recognized the feel of pressed against hers. Instead of savoring the sensation, Valentina shoved at his shoulders, pushing him off. She had to find her babies.

Their babies…

The stroller was still upright, but the girls were crying and reaching out toward her. Fortunately they were strapped in, and while they were scared, they didn't appear harmed. Tears streaked out of Valentina's eyes.

Cash, who'd rolled off her, vaulted to his feet and helped her up. "Are you all right?"

She didn't care about herself; she ran toward her children to check on them. Make sure they were okay. No scratches. No bumps or bruises. So, thank God, the car hadn't struck the stroller at all. Cash must have shoved it out of the way when he'd knocked her down.

"It's okay, it's okay," she murmured to them. Then she turned back toward Cash and asked, "What happened?"

"A black car nearly ran us down," Cash said, but he was speaking into his cell phone, reciting a plate number that he must have somehow been able to read. He wasn't even looking at her. Or the kids.

She didn't want him to; she didn't want him to

see her and definitely didn't want him to get a good look at the girls. Most of all, she didn't want to have to explain what she'd done and why she'd kept the secret for so long.

Right now she just wanted to get herself and her daughters safely away from there, far from that car and ever farther from Cash.

But as she reached for the handle of the stroller, she heard the deep rev of an engine again and the squeal of tires. And she turned and saw that the black car had started back toward them...

Damn it!

How the hell had he missed?

He'd been so close. Too close to give up so soon. No matter that people had called 9-1-1; the police wouldn't get there for a few minutes. So he turned around at the next intersection, scraping cars that were parked along the curb as he made a sharp U-turn to once again face that intersection.

The woman was standing again, right in the middle of the street, next to that big stroller.

Totally focused on his target, he pressed hard on the accelerator and headed straight toward them.

This time he would not miss.

Get 3 FREE REWARDS!

We'll send you 2 FREE Books plus <u>a</u> FREE Mystery Gift.

FREE
Value Over
$20

Both the **Harlequin Intrigue®** and **Harlequin® Romantic Suspense** series feature compelling novels filled with heart-racing action-packed romance that will keep you on the edge of your seat.

HARLEQUIN
PLUS

Try the best multimedia
subscription service for romance
readers like you!

Read, Watch and Play.

Experience the easiest way to get
the romance content you crave.

Start your **FREE TRIAL** at
<u>www.harlequinplus.com/freetrial</u>.